BLOOD RITES

DAVID STUART DAVIES

A Detective Inspector Paul Snow novel

BLOOD RITES

urbanepublications.com

First published in Great Britain in 2017
by Urbane Publications Ltd
Suite 3, Brown Europe House, 33/34 Gleaming Wood Drive,
Chatham, Kent ME5 8RZ

A CIP catalogue record for this book is available from the British Library.

ISBN 978-1-911331-95-7
MOBI 978-1-911331-97-1
EPUB 978-1-911331-96-4

Design and Typeset by Michelle Morgan

Cover by Author Design Studio

Printed and bound by 4edge Limited, UK

In memory of my old friend James Sykes -
a bright light dimmed too early.

'Homosexuals then had three choices.

One. To conform to society's expectations.
To marry and have children.

Two. To be celibate.

Three. To live a double life, fraught with danger – of violence or blackmail – and to live it alone.'

John Fraser in his autobiography *Close Up*

THE END

December 1985

He entered the darkened house and shivered, kicking the damp snow from his shoes. Damn, he thought. He had forgotten to put the central heating on timer. Now, with his antiquated system, it would be a good hour before the property was reasonably warm. He grimaced and slammed the door shut. Oh well, such is life, he mused as he clicked the kitchen switch, filling the room with harsh fluorescent light. After seeing to the central heating boiler, and plugging in the kettle, he went to the sink and extracted the polythene bag from his overcoat pocket. Out of this he unsheathed the long knife. Despite the fact that he had wiped it earlier, the blade still retained traces of blood. He dropped it into the sink and turned on the tap. The water gushed over the knife, the blood reluctantly diluting and then spiralling away. He watched fascinated as the red turned to pink and then slid from view down the plughole.

Well, he supposed the evening had been successful – after a fashion. He wasn't happy that he'd had to deviate from his plan and kill for no other reason than to protect himself. He knew that this had been essential, but it was still a waste of a body. However, the killing did provide him with the opportunity to resume his charted course, his blood rites, and take many more unworthy lives. Needs must when…

He dried the knife on a tea towel and returned it to the kitchen drawer where it belonged. Everything in its place; a place for everything. Sloughing off his wet coat and draping it over a dining chair, he made a cup of tea and, grabbing a couple of chocolate digestive biscuits from the biscuit tin, he wandered into the sitting room. After turning on the television, he slumped in a chair. He took a slurp of tea and sighed. He hoped there was something relaxing and entertaining on the box that he could watch. He'd had rather a tiring evening.

CHAPTER ONE

Three Months Earlier

Paul Snow gazed at himself in the bathroom mirror. He wasn't sure he recognised the man who stared back at him. The features were familiar enough: the long, gaunt face with the prominent nose and unnerving blue eyes, thin taut lips which were forever reluctant to smile and the short cropped hair, fading now to grey at the temples. That was the passport picture Snow, but behind the eyes... What was going on there? What mental turmoil swirled inside that usually focused brain of his? Was he pretending – or simply accepting? Why was he constantly reassessing himself? More importantly, could he live with the metamorphosing Snow? Could he survive, function and still be true to himself? How the hell could he know? The furrows on his brow deepened.

He shut his eyes to blank out the image of his face. Darkness descended and with it more confusion and unease. This bleak reverie was interrupted by the shrill ringing of the telephone. With swift easy moments, relieved to be dragged away from his contemplations, Paul Snow slipped down the stairs and lifted the receiver in the hall.

It was Matilda.

The foyer of the George Hotel was unusually crowded. People had spilled out of the tiny bar and clustered here in groups, engaging in noisy conversation and filling the air with a thin mist of cigarette smoke and the odd raucous laugh. There were one or two men in police uniform – high ranking uniforms – including the Chief Constable; but most of the others wore dinner suits and the women were dolled up to the nines, grinning with pleasure at being given the opportunity to dress extravagantly for once.

When Snow entered with Matilda on his arm, he was confronted with a wall of noise and a blur of faces, most of whom seemed to turn in his direction with interest. He did notice a few of his colleagues give each other a nudge in the ribs and raise an eyebrow. He couldn't blame them. He had attended many of these annual police dinners over the years, but this was the first time he had come along with a woman in tow. His bachelorhood status was much envied by many men on the force, believing, with a kind of teenage naïveté, that not being married meant being in possession of a wild sexual freedom and having no domestic responsibilities. Now it appeared to them that old Snow was about to step into the tender trap and slip on the marital strait jacket.

They had met when Snow had visited the school where Matilda was head mistress during a recent investigation.* Not unsurprisingly, it was she who had made the first move and Snow had not only been flattered and intrigued but strangely found himself prepared to see if such a relationship was possible. This was despite the fact that he realised he was trespassing on alien territory, but he liked Matilda very much as a person at their first meeting and over the intervening few months had grown fond of her.

Snow nodded a greeting at a few acquaintances while guiding Matilda into the bar. Having secured drinks for them after a long wait, they moved back into the foyer.

'Are most of the women here on the force?' Matilda asked quietly.

Snow pursed his lips. 'A goodly number, but there are wives, too.'

'And husbands?'

'Not many. Policewomen either don't survive marriage or they compartmentalise their lives.'

Matilda gave a tight grin. 'I shall have to remember that.'

'I don't believe I've had the pleasure of meeting your lady friend.' A tall man with a mane of thick grey hair, swept back from this broad face, had sidled up to the couple, after gently easing his way through the throng. It was Chief Superintendent Adam Clayborough.

'No, sir. This is Matilda, Matilda Shawcross. Treat her gently. This is the first time she has set foot in the lion's den.'

'Brave girl. Pleased to meet you, Matilda. I'm Adam.'

They shook hands.

'Are you one of Paul's immediate colleagues?' Matilda asked.

'He's my boss,' said Paul.

Clayborough nodded. 'I keep the fellow in check. You have any complaints, report to me, I'll sort it out.' He gave a half wink, but Matilda was not fully convinced by this light-hearted banter. She thought that this imposing fellow actually meant what he was saying. The eyes twinkled, but there was coldness there, too. She sensed a cunning seriousness beneath his smooth bonhomie.

'I think I can handle him,' Matilda responded in the same vein, hating the track this false conversation was taking.

'Why do I get the impression that I've turned invisible?' observed Paul dryly.

'Who said that?' grinned Clayborough, looking around him in mock surprise. And after giving Matilda a full wink this time, he patted Snow on the back. 'Enjoy your evening you two,' he added before turning and merging into the swell of bodies in the room.

'He's a laugh a minute,' said Matilda, with a raise of the eyebrow.

'A good copper but a bit dodgy in the social interaction department. Mind you, I've no room to talk.'

Matilda smiled gently and squeezed his arm.

'To be honest,' Snow continued, 'I hate these occasions. I feel a bit like a fish out of water. I know most of the people here and in the work situation I feel relaxed with all of them, but this is an alien environment to me. Dressed up like a waiter, I'm at a loss.'

Matilda laughed. 'Alien environment? It's the George Hotel, a normal, perfectly respectable establishment! I think it's time for your relaxing pills, Paul.' She squeezed his arm affectionately. 'Come on, sweetie, just go with the flow.' She laughed again and then leaned forward and gave him a gentle kiss on the cheek.

That will certainly get the gossip mongers working overtime, he thought, but said nothing.

For Snow the dinner and the speeches were interminable. The only pleasure he derived from the occasion were the sporadic brief snatches of conversation he had with Matilda when they were not indulging in pedestrian chit chat with their dining companions. As a result, he drank more than he usually did, more than he should, and by the time it came to leave, he realised that he was a little tipsy. It was not a completely new experience for him, although on the rare occasions when it happened, it was usually in the comfort of his own home after a long hard day.

Matilda found his slightly squiffy behaviour amusing and reassuring. It delighted her to see him in such a relaxed state. After going out with Paul for about three months, she was well aware that he had two different personas: the public and the private. Privately, he could be lively, funny and even affectionate at times, but the police strait jacket was donned immediately he had to present himself in any kind of formal situation. She thought of it

as Paul's armour. It puzzled her why he reacted so strongly in this fashion. It wasn't just that he had a public image to project but that he was shielding the real Paul Snow from close scrutiny as though he had something to hide – a dark secret to preserve.

While cotton wool was slowly surrounding his brain and his tongue seemed to have developed a coating which strangely prevented him from enunciating his words clearly, he still managed to keep one small area of his consciousness clear.

'Let's get out of here before I fall down,' he said cheerily.

'With pleasure,' Matilda smiled.

As they rose – Snow somewhat unsteadily – and made their way to the exit, there was a slow general exodus. Snow was by no means the only man there who had drunk more than might be regarded as prudent, especially for a police officer. Indeed, some of the diners were staggering like comic stage drunks.

After they had collected their coats, Matilda guided her charge out on to the street and into the refreshing the cool night air.

'We'll walk up to the station – more chance of getting a taxi there. I'd better see you home.'

Snow nodded. He hated himself for getting like this. Even his bloody legs weren't obeying him as they should. He was moving like a splay-footed penguin. He had been foolish to imbibe so much, but it was the result of his nervousness about taking Matilda to this official shindig, parading her before his colleagues as his girlfriend. There was one dark corner of his mind that kept reminding him of the element of charade in this procedure.

It did not take Matilda long to secure a taxi and within five minutes they were in the back of the cab *en route* for his home.

'I'm sorry about this,' Snow said, his arm waving lazily, the voice thick with alcohol. 'Not like me.'

'Well, that's good. It's time you broadened your horizons.' She grinned and kissed his nose.

'Getting pissed is not exactly broadening my horwizons – horrissons.'

'It's a start.'

As he stumbled out of the taxi, he dug into his coat and extracted a key, which he passed on to Matilda. 'You'd better let us in. I'll not manage the Yale.'

She giggled, paid for the taxi and opened the door. Snow made a bee line for the sofa and slumped down.

'Black coffee for you, my lad,' said Matilda, taking off her coat and draping it over an armchair.

'Yes, please. All the stuff in kitchen.' He flung his arm in the general direction.

It was actually the first time Matilda had been to Snow's house – he'd never quite had the courage to bring her back - but it did not hold any surprises for her. She had already imagined what the place would be like and her assumptions proved to be fairly accurate. It was ultra-tidy, fairly bland and Spartan. There was little personality stamped on the décor, furniture or fittings. She wasn't a detective and she certainly could not have deduced much about the owner of this house just from judging the impersonal interior. It was like a slightly dated show house, as though the occupant had prepared it in order to impress a prospective buyer.

The kitchen gleamed and the work surfaces were free of clutter. She found the instant coffee in a well organised cupboard and brewed two large mugs.

Snow was asleep when she returned to the sitting room. His eyes were closed, his features serene and he was breathing easily as though he was at peace with himself. She gazed down on the man she had been dating for three months with a mixture of gentle emotions. What was she doing with him? He certainly wasn't the easiest person in the world to get to know and yet she found his reticence and reserve rather attractive. He was kind and humorous in her company and possessed a strange kind of magnetism which appealed to her. He was certainly a definite step up from that broad streak of nothing that she had married, the waster she had met at teacher training college. What a disaster that had been. It led to two miserable years and deep emotional scars that scared her off men for years. Indeed, her career became her main focus and that had been more rewarding than any uncertain emotional attachments she might make with a man. Becoming head mistress of St Jude's was the most mentally and emotionally satisfying moment of her life. Matilda was certain that no man could top that. But now she was secure in that role, she began to feel a little lonely. Paul was the first man she had taken a serious interest in since her disastrous marriage. He was tall, interesting and good looking, if you went for gaunt, hollow-cheeked fellows with introspective eyes. But he was hard work. But she liked that. The challenge spiced the relationship for her – a relationship she was more than ready to take to the next level.

She leaned forward and stroked Snow's cheek with her fingers. Her touch roused him and the eyes flickered open. They seemed clearer, more attentive now.

'Sorry about that,' he said pulling himself into a more upright position on the sofa. 'I don't know what came over me.'

'Alcohol,' she said, handing him a mug of coffee.

Snow was grateful. 'Good stuff,' he said, after burning his tongue with his first gulp.

Matilda sat opposite him, cradling her mug as though warming her hands on it. 'Well,' she said, 'that was an interesting evening'.

Snow braved the hot liquid again and took another gulp. The fierce brew seemed to act as a purgative, sweeping away the alcohol fumes from his mind. 'You could say that. 'I'll certainly be the talk of HQ on Monday. Breaking two ducks in one evening.'

'Oh?'

'Taking a lady along to the dinner and getting ... a little worse for wear.'

'Only a little. You didn't jump on the table and sing a rude song or insult the Chief Constable. Nothing like that.'

Snow grinned. 'I am so relieved. Although, if you'd have said I did those things, I reckon I would have believed you.'

'I think it's time you started to live a little more dangerously.'

'I am a policeman, you know. I spend my life chasing criminals. Isn't that dangerous enough?'

Matilda put down her mug in the hearth and crossed to the sofa, sitting next to Paul. 'I'm not talking about your job,' she said bringing her face very close to his. 'I'm talking about you. I'm talking about us.'

Snow's mind cleared further. Sobriety returned. 'I'm not much good in that department. Lack of experience. Wet behind the ears.'

'Well, as a headmistress, I am well placed to give you lessons.' She pressed her body against him and brought her lips close to his.

Snow knew this was the crossroads he'd feared. This was not going to be just a kiss. It was the start of a new stage in their relationship, one that he knew Matilda had been aiming at for quite a while. He was well aware that it was - how could he phrase it? – unnatural in this modern age with two adults in a romantic relationship not to go to bed together. To have sex.

Sex? My God, that word rattled at his cage. He had not had sex with a woman since his early fumblings and uncertainties in his teenage years, before he fully recognised and to some extent accepted his true feelings that would not remain suppressed any more. And he had not had sex at all for… at least ten years. And that had been with a man. Since then, he had been celibate. Forced himself to be celibate for the sake of his career in the force as much as anything. You could not clamber up the promotion ladder if you were a nancy boy.

Matilda had come as a surprise to him. He liked women very much. In fact he felt more at ease in their company than the blokish environment that prevailed at police HQ, but he hadn't actually fancied one since his adolescence when he had felt that he should. It was the done thing for a teenage lad to have a bird on his arm. This was the time before his natural predilections dominated his emotions and threw his life into chaos for a while. He had long since learned that if he was to survive and prosper in his chosen profession, he had to curb all those kinds of thoughts and feelings.

Matilda had attracted him and this threw him into confusion. What complicated matters even more was that she fancied him also. In fact she had made all the running in their relationship and he had just trotted along beside her. He enjoyed her company – there were fewer lonely evenings now – and the fact that he was seen with a woman was good for his image. As a man in his thirties, a confirmed bachelor, it seemed, he knew there were bound to be whispers about him. That is why he had been so careful to ensure that there were no facts.

He had deliberately avoided considering the future, where this innocent little affair would lead. Innocent it was and he was content with the status quo but as Matilda pressed herself even closer to him, unbuttoning his shirt so that she could slip her hand on to his chest, he knew that things were about to change.

She kissed him passionately on the lips. He responded, partly out of pleasure and partly because he knew that was expected of him.

He cursed himself for this play-acting part of his performance. If only he could enjoy the experience as a whole, rather than part of himself standing back, standing at a distance as though viewing the scene with a cool objective eye.

'You'd better show me where the bedroom is,' Matilda whispered in his ear, when they came out of the clinch.

He nodded and smiled at her, while his heart thudded unnervingly in his breast. Now he was fully sober.

Within ten minutes they were naked next to each other in Snow's bed. Her body felt so warm and comforting close to his. He had forgotten the simple pleasure of lying beside someone in the dark. That kind of intimacy was even stronger and more life affirming than sex. Holding Matilda to him, he was reminded how lonely his life was. How he had made his solitary bed and had seemed destined to lie in it alone. And unloved. Now she was here. Next to him. In that solitary bed. It was good. It was comforting.

But it did not arouse him.

He fondled her breasts and then kissed them – but nothing stirred. He knew that the fire of arousal had to come from his emotions not from his brain, not from his intentions but from his desire. In this sense, there was no flame.

Was it nerves? Was it the alcohol? Or was it… well he didn't want to go there. After a while, he knew that nothing was going to happen. Excuses had to be made. Embarrassed and somewhat ashamed he muttered something about having had too much to drink. She was kind and understanding. Maybe, he thought, it was true. But he knew it was a desperate thought. Holding him tightly and kissing him, she told him not to worry or to be upset. In truth, she was not really concerned. She was happy that they had taken a major step forward: ending up naked in bed on the brink of love-making. That was a breakthrough. It clearly indicated the direction in which this affair was heading. Next time it happened, she would make sure Paul was stone cold sober.

CHAPTER TWO

Sometimes Fate sets up a row of dominos and just gives the first one a gentle push and stands back and watches with dark satisfaction the resulting chaos, confusion and tragedy the clattering falling pieces initiate. Certainly this was the case with Barry 'Bazzer' Donovan.

He was the first domino.

If a film producer was making a movie about a disaffected fourteen-year-old from a sink estate, Bazzer Donovan would have been ideal casting. He was small and under-nourished for his age, with narrow deep-set haunted eyes and a feral loping walk. He looked forever furtive and angry. It was an anger that he could not explain. It was just there bonded to his soul and this made him very dangerous. His teachers, his social worker and his mother had all given up on him. There was no reasoning with the creature. He had become a law unto himself, wandering the streets of Deighton at all hours causing problems: stealing, damaging cars, drinking, lighting fires, fighting and taking drugs.

He was particularly disaffected this particular evening. On returning home he found that his stupid mother had gone off to the fuckin' bingo and not left any food in the house. The cow had done it on purpose. The cow! He hated her! The volcanic anger that was always on the verge of erupting within him, spurted forth. He roamed the house smashing up some crockery, ornaments and furniture and then poured a bucket of water on his mother's bed. See how the fat cow liked sleeping on that. He grinned at the thought, but there was no joy or humour there, just malice.

Satisfied that he had done all he wanted in the house, he swept out slamming the door as hard as he could. His anger had not abated. If anything it burned with greater ferocity. He was still hungry and he had no money at all. Not even a few bob to buy his tea at the chippy. Well, he wasn't going to fuckin' starve. He'd just have to get some fuckin' money somehow. And he knew how.

He found himself passing by Wentworth House flats, a multi-story structure built in the Sixties by the council and considered at the time a smart modern housing unit. Now it was a crumbling slum, unloved and in need of demolition. Peeling paint, boarded windows, walls smeared with graffiti and worse, a lift that had not worked in years and was used as a toilet were now the charms of Wentworth House. Only the desperate, the destitute, the serially unemployed and the mentally unstable inhabited this place.

Bazzer saw a lean figure emerge from the building. A tall man, smartly dressed, walking with a swift and urgent step. To Bazzer, he didn't look like one of the inmates of Wentworth House. He was too clean, too upright, too normal. A visitor then. By the look of his clothes, he could be someone from the council, or a doctor or maybe a bleedin' undertaker. They had a lot of deaths in Wentworth House.

Quickening his step, Bazzer caught up with the man.

'Ere mate,' he called, his thin strident tone piercing the silence of the darkened street.

The man stopped in his tracks and turned round.

'Ere mate, I got something for you.'

The man looked quizzically at this strange urchin who had materialised out of the night.

'Yes,' he said.

The next thing the man knew was a sudden harsh pain to his face and a blinding light. He fell to his knees and tried to look up, just as Bazzer hit him again with the half brick. This time he fell back into the gutter, unconscious.

The youth stood over his victim for some time. He was waiting to see if the bastard moved, if he really was unconscious or faking it. Of course, he could be dead. That would be really cool. But no, he could see his chest rise and fall.

Bazzer knelt down by the unconscious man and rifled his pockets. It was slim pickings. Five bob in his trouser pocket and less than a fiver in his wallet.

Fuckin' cheapskate.

He stood up and snarled his disappointment, giving the man a frustrated kick in the ribs. He walked off slowly in the direction of Brian's Chippy.

Some five minutes later, the man regained consciousness and slowly, very slowly, he sat up. He had a thunderous headache and his fingers, gently caressing his forehead, established that he had a cut there and it was still bleeding. Well, at least he was alive. He had to thank God for that.

With infinite care, he pulled himself to his feet and waited a moment while the world around him steadied itself before slowly taking a few steps in the direction of home. There was no sign of his assailant, of course. Well, there wouldn't be, would there? He felt inside his coat to discover that his wallet had gone. He sighed heavily: he was too tired and distressed to swear. Well, he thought, as he made slow progress down the street, there was no point in going to the police. They wouldn't heal his wound or get his money back. He didn't quite know then what a very deep, life-changing impression that brief but brutal encounter with the young brick-wielding hooligan would have on his life and that of others.

The first domino had fallen and the inevitable demolishing process had begun.

CHAPTER THREE

Sometimes there is poetic justice – of sorts. Having secured his fish supper from Brian's chippy, Bazzer slunk out of the shop and meandered down the road, head bent over the steaming paper parcel as he devoured the contents. So concentrated was he on this greasy feast that when he began to cross the road he took no notice of any oncoming traffic. As a result he did not notice the red Vauxhall Cavalier speeding towards him. Behind the wheel was Pete Bramhope who, having consumed several pints at the Red Lion, was well over the legal limit. By his side was his girlfriend Sandra who had encouraged her beau to exceed the speed limit for 'a thrill'. 'Go on, babe, show me a hot pair of wheels,' she had purred, mimicking movie dialogue.

It was a shock to them both when the spindly shape of Bazzer Donovan sprang up before them in the headlights of the car. Before Pete could take any action, Bazzer's body was bouncing off the bonnet of the Cavalier. It cartwheeled in an ungainly fashion over the length of the car before landing face down in the gutter at the far side of the road. Blood trickled from its lifeless mouth and the eyes stared sightlessly at the tarmac littered with the remains of the fish and chip supper.

Bazzer's victim, the man he had attacked and stolen his money in order to buy a fish and chip supper, read of the boy's death in the local paper with great interest. He surprised himself by experiencing a sense of satisfaction and pleasure as he digested the details of Bazzer's violent end. It was as though some unseen force had sought revenge on the boy for all his savage misdemeanours. Indeed, he thought, the world is a better place without the likes of Barry Donovan. This thought sowed a very dark seed in the man's mind.

Some weeks later, Sammy Tindall staggered out of the Almondbury Working Men's Club into a cold winter's night. The pavements were already silvered with frost and a fierce and a bright yellow moon beamed down from a dark cloudless sky. The streets were empty: no pedestrians, no traffic, just the muffled silence hissing in the air. With an ungainly stagger, Tindall slumped with his back against the side wall of the building while he extracted a fag packet and a box of matches from his overcoat pocket and, with the clumsy movements of an inebriate, attempted to extract a cigarette and light it. He giggled at his own incompetence. He found himself enjoying the cumbersome task, the grin broadening on his bleary-eyed face as the match flared into life.

Alcohol brought about strong changes in Sammy's normally dull character: it either made him a clown or a demon. And these could change within seconds. At the moment, as he struggled with matches, fag packet and cigarettes, he was in buffoon mode; but it would not take much to irritate him, arousing the lightly dormant monster within. He could turn nasty in the bat of an eyelid as some of his mates on the shop floor could testify; but with them it was just rough aggression, shouting and foul language – nothing physical. He reserved that kind of abuse for home: for his wife, Brenda. Over the years she had been a regular victim of his beer-fuelled rages, sparked by the simplest of things: his food not ready on time, his favourite shirt not being ironed or simply because he was just in a bad mood. She was at home now, sitting by the fire, cowed and apprehensive. She knew she had to be up, waiting for him to return so that she could make him something to eat, a bacon sandwich or a bowl of soup or whatever demands he made. She daren't go to bed. He would only drag her out of it and unleash his temper on her. She had suffered bruises, black eyes and even a broken arm as a result of his late night rages and recently these had increased in their frequency and ferocity. She lived in fear and hatred of the beast that was her husband. Of course, he was always penitent in the morning when the fumes of alcohol had evaporated. Then came the promises, the bleatings and the tears. It would never happen again. Oh, my God, no it wouldn't. But, of course, it did. One day he will kill me, she thought, and that would be a blessing.

Tindall believed that his outpourings of regret healed any hurt that he had caused Brenda and so his volatile behaviour never really concerned him. The blows came easily and for him they were as easily forgotten. In any case, she made him do it. She deserved it.

Having successfully lit his cigarette and stowed the matches and fag packet away, he staggered forward out of the shadows, and began to make his way downhill towards 3 Hume Royd, his home. Some fifty yards down the road, he saw a figure loitering under a street lamp: a tall silhouette with his head bowed. As Tindall approached, the figure raised his head and turned it in his direction. Although the man's features were in shadow, they somehow seemed familiar to him. He didn't know why, but Tindall sensed this fellow was actually waiting for him, as though they had made some sort of loony assignation to meet under this street lamp. He felt his body tense. Something – he did not know what – was wrong.

The man took a step back, allowing the amber beam of the lamp to illuminate his features.

'You?' croaked Tindall, in surprise, his fag almost falling from his mouth.

'Yes, me,' said the man. 'Hello, Sammy.' The tone was neutral but somehow unnerving to Tindall.

'You're a bit off your beaten track, aren't you?' he found himself saying.

The man shrugged. 'I don't really have a beaten track. Particularly tonight.'

Tindall shook his head, confused. The alcohol lay heavy on his tongue and befogged his brain. He wasn't up to this and really, he felt, as a small spark of anger ignited within him, he didn't have to be. Whatever this smug bastard was talking about and what the fuck he was doing here, did not interest him in the slightest. He was off.

'Good night to you,' he said with something approaching a sneer in his voice. He made to continue his journey, but the man stepped in front of him blocking his way.

'I don't want you to go just yet, Sammy, not until I've given you something.'

'What you talking about?'

'This.'

The man stepped even closer, their faces only inches apart, and then suddenly Sammy Tindall felt a fierce pain in his gut, a pain that seemed to send electric shockwaves to his brain. A fearful incomprehension gripped him. He groaned and gazed down and saw the knife. It glimmered under the streetlight, the blade streaked with blood. With a terrible realisation, he knew it was his blood.

The man stabbed him again, thrusting the knife even deeper this time and turning the handle with great force, slicing upwards through the paunchy flesh. The pain was ferocious, as though his stomach was on fire; but Sammy Tindall's agony was short-lived for very quickly he lost consciousness. He sank down on to the pavement, his eyes and mouth wide open as though in comic surprise. His assailant bent over him and completed the task. Two more deep incisions ensured that the life force had been drained from the body of Sammy Tindall.

The man remained still, crouching by the body for a little while, before rising and sheathing the knife into a plastic bag which he stowed inside his overcoat.

'Good night, sweet Sammy, may angels sing thee to thy rest,' he intoned softly, before moving off swiftly.

CHAPTER FOUR

Paul Snow had only just removed his overcoat and hung it up, when the door of his office opened and DS Bob Fellows bounded into the room.

'Morning, sir. You were saying only last week that things had been a bit quiet recently. Well, you spoke too soon. We've got a dead 'un.'

'There's no need to sound so gleeful, Sergeant. Murdered?'

Bob nodded.

'How?'

'Knifed. Rather nastily.'

Snow reached for his coat. 'Where?'

'Up on the Almondbury estate, near the Working Men's club.'

'OK. Let's go.'

Within minutes, Snow was driving his car from the HQ car park towards the ring road, while Fellows sat beside him with basic notes relating to the murder. 'The victim is forty year old Samuel Tindall. His body was discovered by a late night reveller around midnight.'

'Had he been robbed?'

Bob Fellows shook his head. 'No. His wallet was intact. That's how we were able to identify him so quickly.'

'This late night reveller...'

Bob shook his head again. 'No go there, sir. A young lass. Susan Black. Twenty years old. Missed her last bus from town and couldn't afford a taxi. Apparently she's in a right state. We have her statement – which is no real help.'

'Anything known about this Tindall?'

''Fraid not. No record, if that's what you mean. He's a winder at Parkinson's mill. Married. No kids. Ordinary bloke as far as we can tell so far. Apparently he spent the night in the local Working Men's club. He was well-oiled when he left there quite late. You know how 'flexible' these places are about the licensing hours.'

'I do. But thankfully that's not my concern. Can his wife offer any suggestions as to motive?'

'Not sure. That'll be up to you to ask, I reckon.'

It was a bright October morning. The early mist had cleared and the sun was forcing its way through the clouds. Both ends of Lightfield Road had been cordoned off and a tent had been erected. The forensic team were swarming over the area like albino bees in their special clothing. A small crowd of onlookers had gathered, mumbling amongst themselves, stretching their necks in an attempt to catch some sensational element connected with the police presence.

'Ghouls,' observed Fellows as both men flashed their warrant cards at the constable on sentry duty and slipped under the tape and made their way into the tent. DS Cavanagh greeted them with a grim nod as they entered. 'I think we're just about finished here, sir,' he said, indicating the body bag on the ground. Standing over it with a note book was Chris McKinnon, the forensic officer. 'Morning boys,' he said cheerfully.

Why were these fellows always so damned jolly thought Snow

as he knelt down and unzipped the body bag. A white contorted face stared back at him, with the lower part of the body rich in congealed blood, like a strange scarlet film lying over the clothing. It did not take an expert to see that this had been a violent and vicious attack. There was no doubt whoever had done this wanted the fellow Tindall dead.

'What can you tell me?' Snow asked.

McKinnon shrugged. 'Nothing special. A good number of stab wounds to the midriff, stomach sliced upwards for a several inches. Not expert but extremely effective. The killer was a determined fellow. As far as I can tell at this stage, the victim made no attempt to fight back. There's no sign of a struggle. Too shocked, I guess. No bruises elsewhere and nothing under his fingernails to suggest he fought with his assailant. So it was sudden and, as he was facing the killer, something of a surprise. As to the rest: motive, identity of the culprit etc – the ball's in your court. I doubt if an autopsy will tell us anything more that will be helpful.'

'The weapon?'

'A sharp instrument. Most likely a long knife. Possibly with a serrated edge, like a good kitchen knife. Not much help I know – but then I'm not a clairvoyant.'

With a dramatic gesture, Snow zipped up the body bag. 'Thanks anyway. Best get him out of here then.'

Hume Royd was one of the labyrinthine streets on the homogenous Almondbury estate of post war council houses, built cheaply, quickly and inexpertly. These streets snaked and coiled, interlocking with each other, spreading for nearly a half a mile area of the district: a maze of house upon semi-detached house, all in essence looking the same; slums in embryo, thought Snow.

The door to 3 Hume Royd was opened by a WPC whom Snow had seen around the station but did not know by name. She was young, sturdy and possessing a no-nonsense pugnacity about the eyes which would be very intimidating to the vulnerable. She admitted Snow and Fellows without a word.

'We want to have a chat with Mrs Tindall,' said Snow quietly. 'How is she?'

The WPC shrugged her broad shoulders and pursed her lips. 'Bearing up remarkably well,' she said, the reply heavy with implications. 'She has a visitor with her at the moment...'

Snow raised a questioning eyebrow.

'It's her priest, Father Vincent.'

Snow pursed his lips. 'I'm sure he'll understand we need to talk…'

Taking her cue, the WPC led them to the sitting room where Mrs Brenda Tindall was sitting on the sofa, leaning towards the orange glow of the gas fire, a mug of tea clasped in both hands. Sitting opposite her was a tall, lean man with short cropped hair, which was just beginning to speckle with grey. Snow thought that he had a kind ascetic face, ideal for his calling.

'My apologies for interrupting,' he said. 'I am Detective Inspector Snow and this is my colleague DS Fellows. We need to have a few words with Mrs Tindall.'

The priest leaned forward and touched Brenda Tindall on the shoulders. 'Is that okay with you, my dear?'

She glanced up at Snow and nodded. 'It has to be done sometime,' she said. Her voice was low but it did not waver.

Father Vincent rose and extended his hand to Snow. 'Father Vincent, Thomas Vincent from St Joseph's.'

Snow shook his hand and was surprised how cool it was, as though it had just come out of a refrigerator.

'Brenda and Samuel are part of my flock.'

'Maybe we could have a word later.'

'Indeed,' said Father Vincent before leaving the room, accompanied by the WPC.

Snow sat down across from Brenda Tindall in the same seat that had been occupied by the priest.

'I am sorry to come bothering you at this distressing time, Mrs Tindall, but I need all the information I can get about your husband in order that we can apprehend the person who carried out this terrible deed.' Snow hated these moments where, by a dreadful kind of necessity, he found himself slipping into police-speak, reciting the well-worn rhetoric as though using a cue card.

'It has to be done sometime,' Brenda Tindall said, repeating the phrase in a dull matter of fact fashion. She was a gaunt woman with a yellowish waxy skin. She was probably only about forty but looked older. What surprised Snow was the fact that it seemed to him that she had not been crying. There were no tell-tale signs around the eyes to indicate that tears had been shed. In fact her whole demeanour suggested that she had taken the terrible news of her husband's demise in her stride. From experience, he knew that such shocking news affected people in different ways and it may well be that Brenda Tindall was in denial, unable to accept the truth that her husband was in fact dead – that he would not walk in through the door at any minute. Once the harsh truth had pierced this thin protective screen of self-delusion, the tears would flow.

'Pardon the bluntness of my queries. There is no other way to get to the bottom of this matter and get there quickly'.

'I understand.'

'Have you any idea who might have had such hatred towards your husband that he would want to...' Snow hesitated, not quite sure what was the best, least dramatic phrase to use here: 'kill

him', 'murder him' or maybe 'hurt him badly'. None were really that euphemistic. There really was no way of sweetening the brutal truth.

Mrs Tindall helped him out: 'To top him?' she said flatly. 'Not really. Sammy was not an easy man to get along with and I can't say he had many friends – or any friends really, but I can't think of anyone who felt strongly enough about him to want to murder him. It must be a random killing. A maniac with a knife. A druggie maybe. If you are seeking a motive...' She gave a gentle shrug of the shoulders '... I can't give you one. I can't begin to think of one.'

'You say he was not an easy man. What exactly do you mean?'

'He was moody. You never quite knew which Sammy he would be each day.'

'How long have you been married?'

'About fourteen years now, I reckon. You lose track.'

'Was it a happy marriage?'

To Snow's surprise, Brenda Tindall laughed. 'And how would you describe a happy marriage, Inspector? He didn't bring me champagne and flowers and there were no roses around the door if that's what you mean but… we rubbed along.'

'You have no children.'

She shook her head. 'No… he… Sammy didn't want them.'

'What about you?'

This questioned seem to puzzle her for a moment and then she shook her head. 'No,' she said quietly and the first time there was a hint of sadness in her eyes. She leaned forward and placed her mug into the tiled hearth, as she did so the sleeve of her cardigan pulled back revealing her wrist and lower forearm. Snow noticed the dark marks there.

'Your husband was at the working man's club last night. Did he go there often?'

'A couple of nights a week maybe.'

'Did he take you?'

'What for?'

'A night out.'

'It's a working man's club. I'm not a working man.'

Snow could see he was well and truly down the cul de sac now and the end was in sight.

'Is there anything you could tell us that may help in our investigation, in our attempt to catch the man who… murdered your husband.'

Mrs Tindall did not have to think before she replied. 'No,' she said. 'As I said, it must have been a madman, one of these crazy folk you read about. No one we know or owt.'

Snow rose from his chair. 'Thank you, Mrs Tindall. We'll leave you now but no doubt we'll speak again. Do you have any friends or relatives who can stay with you for a few days to help you during this difficult time?'

'I will be all right. I've rung my sister in Manchester. We're not close but she's going to get over here tomorrow, but I can manage.'

Snow believed her. 'It will be necessary for you to make a formal identification of the body in the near future. Do you think you will be able to cope with that?'

'Of course.' Was there a hint of a smile on that tired, waxen face? Snow thought so and the sight of it chilled him.

In the hall, Father Vincent and the WPC were engaged in a casual hushed conversation. They broke off and turned to face Snow and Fellows.

'All finished?' enquired the priest.

'For the moment, Father. You said that the Tindalls were part of your flock…'

The priest nodded.

'They were regular churchgoers?'

Father Vincent smiled indulgently. 'I'd hardly say that. In fact in these days we have very few 'regulars' in the sense that they attend all my services or become familiar faces in the congregation. It's a sign of the times, I'm afraid. There are so many calls, temptations if you like, on people's times these days. But the Catholic conscience catches them from time to time and obliges them put in an appearance.'

'Is that what the Tindalls did?'

Father Vincent hesitated a moment before replying. 'You could say that.'

'How well do you know the couple?'

The priest's shoulders rose in a gentle shrug. 'Not well, at all. A casual conversation, nothing very deep. It is really moments like this, moments of crisis, when the priest is able to get close, is able to be of real help.'

'Was it your impression that they were a happy couple?'

The priest gave a wry grin. 'Oh, it would, I think, be dangerous, inappropriate at least, to talk about my impressions. That's not fact is it? Not evidence. Impressions don't really count.'

'They can point the way to the truth.'

'Or elsewhere. In the opposite direction, for example. Tell me, Inspector, why do you ask?'

'Impressions.' It was now Snow's turn to give a wry grin. 'Mrs Tindall seems quite stoical about her husband's death…'

'Grief affects us in many ways.'

'Indeed it does, but you usually get a sense of…imminent despair. The notion that they can't or won't believe what has happened. Mrs Tindall seems fully secure in her understanding that her husband has been murdered. It does not seem to have rocked her boat in any serious fashion. And then there are the bruises on her arm. To my eye they looked as though they were inflicted.'

'Oh, dear.'

'Had you heard that perhaps Mr Tindall was a violent man? A violent man at home?'

'It's not within the parameters of my calling to deal in matters of rumour, Inspector. Shall we leave it at that?'

'Did she raise the matter with you at all?'

'If she did, that would have been a very private and confidential conversation.'

'In the case of murder, nothing is confidential. Are you saying that Mrs Tindall admitted her husband's violent behaviour towards her in a confessional?'

'I am not saying that at all. It would be beyond my vows as a priest to say it. You should know that, Inspector. What transpires between a priest and a parishioner in the confessional is sacrosanct. That is the whole nature of the process.'

Snow nodded. Although the priest was playing the clam, his prevarications had only strengthened his suspicions. 'Thank you, Father,' he said, politely. 'We'd better be on our way.'

'May God go with you and help you in your endeavours.'

'Talk about brick walls, eh,' muttered Fellows as they walked back towards the car.

'Yes, well I've encountered the sealed lips of the clergy before. It's nothing personal; they just believe it's not their role in life to gossip.'

'Gossip!'

'Pass on rumours and impressions. But nevertheless, I reckon we can gather there was no real affection between the Tindalls and if my assumptions are right about those bruises, we may have a wife beater on our hands.'

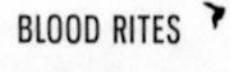

'Or on the slab in the morgue, to be precise.'

Snow gave a bleak smile. 'How absolute the knave is'.

Bob Fellows, ignorant of the quotation, chuckled. 'If you say so, sir.'

'Well, that leads to a little job I've got for you. Have a chat with the neighbours roundabout. See what they have to say about the Tindalls, Sammy in particular. I'm sure they will not be as reticent as Father Vincent to spill any juicy beans. Get a taxi back to HQ.'

'OK, sir.'

'In the meantime, I'll see what they have to say about our victim at the working man's club. We'll have a conflab over coffee in my office this afternoon. Wheels will be in operation for me to make a statement to the media. No doubt the telly folk will want something. Oh, how I hate those bloody circuses.'

With a furrowed brow and a gloomy look, Snow got back into his car.

CHAPTER FIVE

'It's not so much that the trail has gone cold, it was never really warm in the first place, sir.'

It was a week later and Snow had been called into Chief Superintendent Clayborough's office for a progress report on the Tindall investigation. Little had happened and there had been no real developments. The murder had been widely reported in the local press and on the regional television news programmes and briefly had made it into the national newspapers – somewhere around page six. As Snow explained to Clayborough, there were no indications as to motive and there was no one in the frame as the culprit. It seemed to have all the hallmarks of a random killing, as Brenda Tindall had observed, 'made by one of those crazy people you read about.'

Snow gave his boss a succinct but fairly comprehensive breakdown of the minutiae of the case. Clayborough appeared to listen intently, but Snow knew that he was merely following procedure in asking for this update. He was experienced enough to realise that when one was presented with a case like this – a mystery murder with no clues as to who committed it or why - there was little one could do but keeping turning over the meagre pickings one had until something turned up. And one had to hope that the 'something' was not another body.

'Very well, Paul,' Clayborough said at last when Snow had finished. 'It's a bit of a bugger, but I reckon you're the best man to handle such a case. Any breakthrough, keep me informed.'

'Yes, sir.' Snow turned to go, but Clayborough sat forward in his chair, leaning on his desk, his arm raised in a gentle accusative gesture.

'By the way, you're a dark horse, aren't you?'

Snow raised a quizzical brow.

'That lovely young lady you were with at the George the other night. You've kept her under wraps, haven't you?'

Snow did not know how to respond. He wanted to say, 'Mind your own bloody business,' but discretion easily conquered his growing irritation.

'Is this serious?'

Snow now wanted to punch him. 'It's… it's early days, sir.'

'I must say she looked rather too lovely to let go. Delightful girl. You know, Paul, I like my officers to be married. The home life that marriage brings gives a fellow a broader, a more perceptive view on life, on society, and as such makes them a more effective officer. This is a tough old job. It can be a bitch at times and it is useful to have someone to go home to and soothe the old furrowed brow. There's something about the security of marriage that gives one a cushion against the old slings and arrows. An empty house gives no solace. I've been married twenty three years and I'm sure I wouldn't be where I am today, if I hadn't had the love and support of my wife.'

Snow gave what he hoped was an understanding nod. 'I'll remember that.'

The two men looked at each other for some seconds before Snow moved infinitesimally towards the door.

'Is that all, sir?'

Clayborough gave a tight smile. 'Yes, that's all.'

Taking the lift down from the top floor, Snow whispered as many foul expletives as he could, repeating 'the fucking interfering bastard' numerous times. Why did these bloody high ups think they had the power to interfere in the lives of their officers, like a bloody puppet master. The interview was a brutal reminder that the top brass kept their minions under close scrutiny at all times, even their personal life. With this in mind, Snow realised with unease, it was no wonder his secret had remained so. Or had it? Was Clayborough's bluster about Matilda lightly just veiled encouragement - or warning, even - to legitimise his sexuality? He sighed heavily. Or maybe he was being paranoid again?

By the time he reached his office, Snow was desperately trying to put the memory of his interview with Clayborough and its imagined repercussions out of his mind and return his mental focus back to the Tindall murder. He made himself a strong coffee and sat at his desk and began to review the case once more.

It was now clear that Tindall was guilty of domestic violence. Although Mrs Tindall had revealed nothing, two of her neighbours had told tales of black eyes, a broken arm and sounds of fierce shouting and screams heard through the walls of the semi. Her doctor had also confirmed that she had been treated for injuries, the cause of which he regarded as suspicious, although he had no strong grounds for taking the matter further. Interviews with Sammy Tindall's work colleagues and the shop floor foreman confirmed that he was moody and easily irritated, but that his aggression was restricted to abusive words and snarled expletives. Typical of the cowardly breed, it seemed, he reserved his violent outburst for the vulnerable and easily cowed: his wife. That, of course, as Bob Fellows emphasised with enthusiasm, gave Brenda Tindall a strong motive and placed her in the frame for murder. Snow knew he was right in theory but he was not convinced by this simplistic solution. The forensic evidence tended to provide a stumbling block for this theory anyway. The angle of the knife wounds entered the body indicated that the culprit was someone approaching six feet tall. Mrs Tindall was barely five foot four.

Nevertheless, it was clear that Mrs Tindall felt no real sadness at the death of her husband. There had been no tears, no breakdown, and no emotional expressions of loss and despair. The previous day Snow had attended Sammy's funeral, mainly in order to observe if there were any strangers present eager to gloat over their handiwork. But there had been no ghoulish spectres at the feast. It was a small affair with a few neighbours in support of Brenda, her sister, the secretary of the working men's club and a representative from his works. A sad end to a sad life.

However, what had been most revealing to Snow was the dramatic change in Brenda Tindall herself. She had turned up in a smart black outfit, glamorous widow's weeds, her face carefully made up and the hair that had been mousy and straggly now honey coloured and beautifully coiffured. It was a transformation worthy of one of those wretched TV make over shows. But it wasn't only her appearance that was different. Her manner and bearing were assured and serene. She was a changed woman. She had escaped the shackles of her violent, loveless marriage and had become the person she had always wanted to be. It was a remarkable transformation and certainly revealed that she was in possession of more steel and guts than the sad stoical creature he had first interviewed. Could she have done it? Could she have really butchered her husband to escape from his abusive clutches? His instinct told him no, but he knew that he could not ignore the possibility altogether. He had to keep this notion on the back burner while investigations continued.

While investigations continued? Well, they had come to a full stop. There were no avenues left to travel down. Sammy's workmates and employer had been questioned, as had the barman and some of the regulars at the working men's club who had been in attendance on the night of the murder. They had all told the same story: he was a bit of a difficult devil at times but no real trouble. They knew of no one who bore any kind of serious grudge. He seemed content with his own company and that night at the club, he had sat alone reading the paper apparently lost in in his own thoughts while getting steadily drunk. Snow kept coming back to the inevitable conclusion that the only person he knew who had benefitted from Sammy Tindall's death was Sammy Tindall's wife. Fellows' theory in a nutshell. Snow could not fully explain why he rejected this notion, but he knew that this was not the case. He felt it down to the roots of his policeman's soul. It hung on that one point: 'the only person he knew who had benefitted from Sammy Tindall's death'. Snow was convinced that there was – somewhere out there – a person he *didn't* know. The mystery man. The tall person with the serrated knife who had some sort of grudge against wife-beating Sammy. He had considered the possibility of Mrs T having a boyfriend in the shadows who had taken it upon himself to ease the situation, to cut her free; but there was no evidence whatsoever to support such a theory at the moment. There was no homicidal paramour lurking in the shadows. Of course it would be a situation that he would monitor but he reckoned if there had been another bloke they would have got a sniff of him by now.

Wouldn't they?

Snow gazed down at his notepad. It was filled with geometric doodles. He sighed. Those were not going to help him solve the case.

CHAPTER SIX

Mandy Sullivan was shaking as she entered the toilet cubicle. Her eyes pricked with tears and her mouth was dry, her tongue seeming an alien part of her. 'Oh, God, Oh God,' she thought in desperation. 'Help me now. Please!'

She sat on the loo and with some difficulty she tore open the packet and extracted the contents. With her heart thumping wildly in her breast, she just stared down at the stick she was grasping in her hands. Frozen with fear and apprehension, for some moments she could not move while the stick wavered in an out of focus. She was shaken from this trance by shrieks and giggles as a couple of girls banged their way into the loo. She recognised their voices: they were classmates. Their natural uninhibited exuberance pierced her heart. Once she had been like them: carefree and happy. And normal. Before the nightmare had taken complete hold of her life. She bit her lip as copious tears spilled down her cheeks. The girls, oblivious of her presence, entered nearby cubicles and kept on chatting while they had a pee.

Mandy waited until they made their noisy exit. Quickly she re-read the instructions on the back of the packet and then, still with trembling hands, carried out the procedure. She closed her eyes and prayed. In this instance the prayers were not answered – not in the way she desired.

The stick had turned blue. As she had feared it would.

She felt as though someone had kicked her hard in the midriff and she felt the bile in her stomach rise. Her head fell back against the tiled wall. 'Oh, my God,' she cried out loud. Her world had just crumbled into dust and she was alone. There was no one, no one she could confide in. No one.

The Asian shopkeeper looked at Mandy suspiciously as she placed the bottle of vodka on the counter. She had plastered herself with makeup, heavy eyeliner, bright red lipstick – the lot – in order to look older than her fifteen years. She could see that he was about to say something about an ID but she was determined to brazen things out. If he started to become awkward she'd just run out of the shop with the vodka, certain that this old bloke wouldn't be able to catch up with her. Before the shopkeeper had a chance to say anything, she flashed him the twenty pound note before placing it on counter next to the bottle. He gave a little sigh. What did it matter if this young scrap of a girl wanted to ruin her life and her looks with booze? It was none of his business. His business was to sell the stuff. He placed the bottle in a flimsy plastic bag and scooped up the note. Moments later, with the change jingling in her pocket and a bottle of vodka clasped tightly in her hands, Maureen left the shop, wearing a sour grin on her heavily made up face.

An hour later, Maureen was huddled up in a corner of one of the shelters in Greenhead Park, about a mile from the town centre. She had consumed half the bottle of vodka, but instead of relieving the terrors of her situation, the alcohol had exacerbated them. It was not just the oncoming evening chill that made her body shudder and her lips chatter. It was fear. Fear that had clamped itself around her consciousness and would not let go. Every time she closed her eyes to blot out reality, she experienced the same sensations over again like the running of a film in her head. She remembered the casual touches, the stroking of her breasts, the hand in her knickers, the walking in on her in the bathroom. Those images flashed by, a speedy prologue, before…

She remembered lying in her bed, her body rigid with stomach-turning apprehension. Every noise terrified her. Those clicks and snaps were the normal sounds of a house settling for the night. Or were they? Was that gentle bumping noise the sound of the central heating radiators shutting down for the night of was it the stealthy tread of footsteps coming up the stairs, coming towards her room?

And then she heard the door handle turn and a thin shaft of pale light arrow its way into the room. It disappeared as quickly as it arrived, but it had announced the dreaded presence by her bed.

'Hello, darling,' he whispered. Two words, two words uttered with a drunken drawl that turned her blood to ice. She screwed her eyes shut, daring not look as she heard him move closer. Soon his boozy breath was on her face and he kissed her cheek.

'No,' she said softly, so softly it could have been a sigh.

He pulled back the covers of the bed and slipped in beside her. He was naked from the waist down and she felt his warm flesh press hard against her.

'Come on, darling,' he said, pulling her round towards him. 'There's a good girl.'

She tried to utter the word 'No' again but this time she could not speak. Her mouth moved mechanically but no sound was uttered. Fear had silenced her.

'You're a lovely girl, my darling,' he said thickly, pulling her knickers down her legs, his fingers rough against her smooth skin, and then with a groan of satisfaction, he slipped his hand between her thighs. She moaned. It was a gentle bleat of disgust and horror but he interpreted it as one of pleasure. 'That's it,' he gurgled.

And then before she knew it, he was on top of her and penetrating her. This is where the memory became very distorted. She remembered the ferocity, the harsh rhythm and the agonising pain as he pounded down on her, but even at the time it seemed to be happening to someone else. It couldn't be happening to me, she thought, desperately trying to believe that this was some horrific nightmare. She did, however, remember his exclamation of pleasure and the final shudder, but then she had no recollection of him dragging himself off her or leaving the room. It was all darkness then. Pain, disbelief and darkness. Her fragile mind sought refuge in sleep.

The pain was still there in the morning as shards of bright sunlight pierced through the gaps of her curtains. A new day and a new cruel reality. It had happened. To her. She had been raped. She had been raped by her father. It had been coming for some time and now it had really happened. The drunken monster had taken her virginity. She could still feel him inside her. The thought of it made her vomit. Green bile spattered her bed clothes as her body shook with silent crying.

As it did now, in the park shelter. As it always did when she recollected that terrible night. Which was often. She could not shake it from her mind. That face. The pain. The invasion of her body.

And now the final agony: she was pregnant. With his child. With the monster's child. Her own father's offspring. She was a freak. It was unbearable.

She cried out loud. It was a feral cry, a mixture of despair and anger. Snatching up the vodka bottle she took another long hard gulp. The alcohol burned her throat. That was good. She wanted to feel physical pain to divert her from her mental anguish.

She slumped back on the wooden bench, woozy and distraught. What on earth was she to do? Who could she turn to? And then she had an idea.

CHAPTER SEVEN

Paul Snow pulled up outside a smart modern detached house in the Lindley area of Huddersfield. It was, he knew, what was commonly referred to as the Yuppie belt. The houses here were a cut above those on the new cheek-by-jowl estates which had postage stamp gardens, garages too narrow to use for cars and cheap utilitarian fittings. This particular house was but one of six, all slightly different on a 'select development' called Primrose Rise. It amused Snow that builders chose such airy-fairy names in order, no doubt, to suggest a pastoral haven, a rural backwater of delights, the haunt of deer, rabbit and rare butterflies. In this case the nearby sodium street light and the bus shelter at the end of the street banished any notion of Hardyesque tranquillity.

Three Primrose Rise was the home of Matilda Shawcross and Snow had been invited to dinner. He had been to her house before but only for the purpose of picking Matilda up to go on elsewhere. This was the first time he would sample her hospitality. Hospitality. He considered the word carefully. He was fully aware of the implications that it held on this occasion. A few weeks had elapsed since his failed attempt to make love to her and although the event had not been referred to specifically, by either of them, he knew that Matilda was – how was he to consider this? 'encouraged' was perhaps the best word - encouraged that things would develop very soon. And, he reckoned, that tonight, she was going to provide him with the opportunity for this to happen. He had been aware that this was a likely outcome right from the very beginning when he had first started seeing Matilda. He had tried to ignore the inevitability of such an event, despite him knowing that any relationship with an attractive woman was bound to lead to a physical relationship – unless there was something wrong with one or both of them.

Of course, in this instance, he thought sourly, there was something wrong with one of them. In a sense, at least. He gazed at himself in the driving mirror, his features illuminated by the soft green glow of the dashboard. He looked like some horror creature from a Hammer film. The thought amused him briefly and his mouth curled into a gentle smile. He was not unaware of the various ironies of his situation. For a start many a red-blooded man would relish with great enthusiasm romping amongst the bed clothes with Miss Matilda Shawcross. She was a very attractive woman. Also, it had been in his power to allow this relationship to falter and then end before it reached this crucial stage. He had, after all, made a point to the outside word that staid bachelor Snow had the ability and inclination to attract a beautiful woman. But what really bothered him and kept him awake at night was the gnawing belief that it was all a sham. He was not only pretending to the world but also to Matilda and worse, to himself. He had successfully repressed his homosexual feelings and activities for almost ten years now in order to pursue a successful career in the police force where puffs, shirt-lifters, bum boys and queers were seen as a sniggering joke, a threat, open to blackmail; and certainly did not rise in the ranks.

Now, here he was playing the straight man. He tried to convince himself that his feelings had changed, had mutated. He had matured and was now ready for a 'normal' relationship. One with a woman. He despised himself for thinking in terms of 'a normal relationship' but he was indoctrinated by the society he was part of to view the matter in this way. He had to try but he felt guilty that such a lovely and trusting creature as Matilda was his guinea pig. Maybe… maybe it would have a happy ending.

He had psyched himself up for this evening, tried to prepare both mentally and physically. There would be kissing and love making and he would prove himself a 'normal man'.

There would be a happy ending.

He switched off the lights, grabbed the bottle of Chablis and the flowers from the back seat of the car and headed for the front door. He felt strangely calm and determined as he rang the doorbell. He heard the gentle chimes echo in the house. Moments later, Matilda opened the door, a broad smile on her face.

'Hello, Paul,' she said softly, leaning forward to kiss him.

Mandy Sullivan returned to the hiding place where she had stashed the bottle of vodka, or what was left of it. She held it up close to her face. Fuck, there was barely an inch left. She unscrewed the top and gulped it all down. God, it was good. She needed a drink after her recent experience. That had been a waste of time. No bloody help there then. She wandered down through the town centre towards Aspley and the canal.

She had a plan. Of sorts. A kind of solution. She giggled bleakly at this word. As the alcohol swirled around in her brain, she mouthed the word, 'solution', to her amusement, the breath escaping from her mouth in a fine grey cloud. The numbing effects of the vodka had protected her from the growing cold and despite the thin coat she was wearing, she was oblivious of the night chill. She turned off the road, staggered unsteadily down the steps and on to the tow path. She gazed at the canal for some moments as though mesmerised by it. The water, she thought, looked like black treacle, dark with an occasional bright spot created by the moonlight.

She drained the vodka bottle dry and then hurled it into the air. It arced over the water before dropping down, making a muted splash before sinking into the murky depths without trace. She thought of the phrase 'without trace' and as with the word 'solution', she mouthed it aloud to herself. That's where she wanted to be: without trace. Lost to the world. Me and the monster's baby inside of me. Then the bastard would be sorry. His daughter floating in the bloody canal. His impregnated daughter. Dead. And all his fault. Well, she reasoned, in her drunken stupor, it was for the best. There was no other alternative. She was ruined, scarred, blighted for life now. They would say that she had led him on – seduced the monster. She was a whore. There really was no future for her.

She made her way towards the edge of the path and stared down defiantly at the dark, reedy waters. Suddenly, she felt terrified at the thought of what she was about to do. The fear sobered her a little. She knew that she couldn't do it. I am just not brave enough, she told herself, shaking her head wildly. Or am I being stupid? Oh, God I don't know. She began to cry, loudly this time, great vociferous sobs. Her body was wracked with emotion, tears blinding her vision. She jerked forward in her anguish and missed her footing. The ground slipped away from her and she found herself falling. For a moment the world seemed to spin round, darkness and moons flashing by and then the icy water engulfed her. She was plunged down deep into its thick blackness, the ferocious, unyielding cold paralysing her limbs. Her mouth and nostrils filled with the foetid water as she desperately tried to reach for the surface but some invisible force seemed to hold her down. Her leg scraped against some unseen sharp object, the pain shooting up her body. With one desperate effort she reached her arm upwards and for a split second her hand broke the surface of the waters but she was pulled down again by the undertow, deeper this time into the reedy maw of the canal. Her movements faltered and her brain began to shut down. She no longer struggled against her fate. She couldn't and now, strangely, she didn't want to. As her lungs filled with water and the life eased its way from her, the body of Mandy Sullivan rose slowly to the surface of the canal as though it was releasing her back to the world.

Paul Snow sat in bed, propped up by a pillow, while he drank a mug of strong hot coffee. There was a gentle smile playing about his lips but this reflected his sense of relief rather than humour. He had succeeded. He had been a man. Lying by his side, with sleepy, contented eyes, was Matilda. For her the evening had gone exactly as she had hoped, exactly as she had planned. Her silence exuded contentment. She was happy to be in a relationship with a decent man who was kind, considerate and intelligent. She knew that it was not a romance of cinematic proportions: there were no sweeping strings or tinkling bells. But what the hell, this was real life and one had to snatch what happiness one could get. After a moment she leaned over and kissed Paul on the cheek. He responded in kind.

Paul had found the whole experience slightly surreal. During the act of making love, it was almost as though he had been able to step out of his own body and stand back and watch. This was not for any prurient sensation but rather with a strange sense of curiosity and analysis. Because this was a unique occasion, he wasn't sure whether he had enjoyed it or not. His main concern had been to please Matilda, to not let her down again and in the process prove to her, to himself, to the world that he could be a man. To indulge in a normal heterosexual act. It seemed that he had succeeded in mechanical terms at least, much to his surprise and relief. Where this left him now he was not sure, but he had made a step along a new strange road and there were no longer any sign posts.

CHAPTER EIGHT

Frank Sullivan had only just got in from work when there came a knock at the door. Glancing through the sitting room window he saw the two police officers, a man and a woman, and he knew immediately that it was something to do with Mandy. She hadn't come home the night before and although this wasn't completely unusual – she occasionally stayed at a school friend's house – he had sensed that this was not the case on this occasion. Things had been difficult over the last few months since that night. That night he now desperately regretted.

'Mr Frank Sullivan?'

His stomach tightened into a hard knot at the sight of the two uniformed officers on his doorstep. They were youngsters, not yet over thirty, fresh faced and solemn. The man had an incipient moustache, grown, thought Sullivan, to make him look older. It simply made him look comical.

He nodded dumbly.

'May we come in, sir?'

Without a word, Sullivan turned on his heel and the policemen, removing their helmets followed him into the front room.

'Is it Mandy?' he said, his voice flat and dry. 'Has she got herself into some kind of trouble?'

The two policemen exchanged embarrassed glances. They were

not used to this kind of assignment.

'I'm afraid we have some bad news, sir,' said the officer with the moustache and then he gave a little nervous cough as he examined his boots.

The young woman took over, 'A body was discovered in the Huddersfield canal this morning,' she said, almost in a whisper. 'A young girl. We believe it to be your daughter.'

Sullivan shook his head in bewilderment. The words didn't make sense. 'In the canal?'

'Drowned'

'Drowned? You mean she's dead?' he found himself saying, as his legs began to give way and he slumped down into the armchair.

Both police officers nodded, not quite brave enough to give a vocal assertion.

After a brief pause, the WPC continued. 'We found her handbag in the water near where her… near her …which gave us her identity.'

'We think she had been drinking and… had fallen in,' the policeman added.

'Oh, my God.' Sullivan hid his face in his hands and his body shook with emotion. He felt like someone had thumped him hard in the stomach and had winded him. He could hardly breathe. His breath escaped in a strangled squeak from his constricted lungs. The two officers stood by awkwardly and waited until he brought his emotions under control. Eventually, he turned his tear-stained face up towards them, a dim light of desperation in his red-rimmed eyes. 'Are you sure it's my Mandy?'

'Well, we'll need you to make a formal identification, but it seems most likely, sir. I am very sorry,' said the WPC, reaching out and placing a comforting hand on Sullivan's shoulder.

Suddenly Sullivan began to shiver. It was though all his blood had turned to ice and a fierce chill had invaded his body. This can't be happening, surely, his brain suggested. Maybe he was dreaming. The thought evaporated along with all hope as he gazed up at the serious faces of the two officers.

'What about Mrs Sullivan?' asked the policeman.

'There isn't one,' replied Sullivan, dragging his sleeve across his face to wipe his tears. 'I mean she's gone. Left. Years ago.'

'Where is she now?'

He shook his head. 'I've no idea. Timbuktu for all I know or care. She walked out on us a long time back. She'll not be interested in what's happened to Mandy.' The mention of his daughter's name brought the horror of the situation back to him and he began to cry again.

'Drowned,' he said softly. 'My little girl drowned.'

Later that day Frank Sullivan identified his daughter in the white tiled, antiseptic smelling morgue. The green sheet was pulled back to reveal the pale bloated face of a young girl, his daughter. He leaned forward to gaze at her features in the harsh light. She looked like a parody of her real self, those wide staring eyes and puffy cheeks. This wasn't Mandy. It was a wax doll. A pretend Mandy. Tears clouded his vision and he turned away.

The other two people in the room, DS Sandra Morgan and Dr Raymond Simpkins, the senior pathologist, waited patiently for Sullivan to give them confirmation that the body on the slab was indeed his daughter Maureen.

'Yeah, it's her,' he said at last, the words tearing his heart in two, as though they were responsible for her death and not the dark waters of the canal.

'So sorry for your loss, Mr Sullivan,' said Sandra stepping forward, ready to lead him away, but Dr Simpkins raised his hand gently to stop them.

'Did you know that your daughter was pregnant?'

The words were yet another hammer blow to Sullivan's system and he felt the bile rush into his throat and his body began to crumple.

Sandra flashed an accusative glance at the pathologist. The old goat should have waited before imparting this news. Had he no sensitivity? This was neither the place nor the time to tell the chap that his fifteen year old daughter was up the duff.

'That can't be right,' said Sullivan, shaking his head.

'I'm afraid it is. She was three months gone. Presumably there was a boyfriend on the scene,' said Simpkins.

Sullivan wanted to scream. He couldn't bear the pain, the despair, the guilt. He staggered a few steps forward and looked as he was about to faint.

Sandra Morgan stepped forward and grabbed his arm firmly, steadying him. 'Let's get you somewhere you can have a sit down with a nice cup of tea.'

Fifteen minutes later Sullivan was seated in a cubbyhole of an office with a mug of tea and smoking a much needed cigarette. Opposite him with a case folder on her knee was DS Morgan.

'I am sorry that you had to find out about your daughter's pregnancy in such a fashion. I could see from your reaction that you had no idea about it.'

'No. Nothing.'

'She had a boyfriend?'

Sullivan shook his head. 'No. Nobody.'

Sandra pursed her lips. 'Well, sorry to be blunt about this, but there must have been somebody.'

Sullivan eliminated that statement from his consciousness as soon as it had been uttered.

‘Are they sure? Could there be some mistake? She was a good girl.’

Sandra was tempted to observe that it was usually the good girls who get caught out. The bad girls are savvy and use protection. But she was aware that imparting this piece of wisdom at this time would be rather insensitive and certainly would not help matters. ‘I’m sorry,’ she said quietly. ‘There is no mistake.’

Sullivan gave a weary shrug of the shoulders. ‘Well, I’m sorry. I can’t help you. I have no idea who the father is,’ he lied.

‘There is one other point I wish to raise with you Mr Sullivan,’ said Sandra.

Sullivan tensed again. What now? What bloody now?

‘I am sorry to have to mention this, but it is important that I do. You appreciate that we have to take into consideration all kinds of possibilities in this matter. Here we have a young girl, under age, three months pregnant and with, as you now tell us, no regular boyfriend. It could be that in despair, Maureen may have committed suicide.’

‘No.’ The word emerged as an elongated moan and Sullivan slumped back in his chair.

‘However painful it is for you to accept this scenario, I am afraid it is a realistic one. To find oneself pregnant at that age with no father of the child on the scene is traumatic to say the least. She was three months into the pregnancy and obviously she had not confided in you, her dad. She was probably too scared to. She had been drinking – a considerable amount of alcohol had been found in her system. The effect of the drink may well have clouded her reasoning. All these aspects could easily lead to her taking her own life. In her situation it may have seemed the only option.’

Sullivan slumped back in his chair, gently shaking his head. Not only was he lost for words but he was also lost for emotion.

The dramatic and gut wrenching events of the last few hours had finally exhausted his emotional reserves. He was just a husk, all passion spent.

As dusk fell that day, Frank Sullivan sat on the sofa in the gloom of his sitting room nursing a bottle of whisky. The only illumination to counteract the thickening evening shadows was the glow of the gas fire which hissed seductively at him from the tiled hearth. He felt wretched – wretched on so many counts that he could not fully isolate them. They were all bunched together in one coagulated tight ball of misery. He had lost his daughter and she may well have killed herself because of what he had done to her. One of God's greatest sins: incest. And it seemed that he had fathered a child by his own child. And he was, therefore, responsible for its death also. He was dammed: a walk over hot coals to purgatory was his. What had made him do it? What had made him desire his own daughter. Lust? Loneliness? Alcohol-fuelled depravity? All those things and more.

The simple truth that kept returning to his brain like a red hot branding iron was that he was an evil man. He had to accept that fact that he must suffer. He had to if there was any chance of some kind of redemption in this life. God knew what he was like. God would have seen his terrible transgression: spilling seed inside his own flesh. God was now punishing him. And he had to accept it. He took another large swig of whisky straight from the bottle, its glass neck clinking hard against his teeth. How was he going to cope with life now? With the guilt? That dark indelible blemish on his soul. One thing was for sure, the bottle was not helping. It was nearly empty and he felt far from drunk. The alcohol had neither eased his pain nor helped to eradicate the guilt. How could it? Booze cannot change the truth. In a violent gesture, he cast the bottle aside, the remaining liquid splashing onto the carpet. Curling up into a foetal ball on the sofa, clasping his arms over his head, he groaned and sobbed, praying that sleep would overtake him and provide some respite from his physical and mental agony.

CHAPTER NINE

Paul had not seen Matilda for almost a week. The various duties of their respective careers had meant that meeting up often proved difficult. There had been a few telephone conversations and then an evening drink had been arranged at the last minute at the Nag's Head, a pleasant hostelry a couple of miles from town. Paul had missed her company. She was one of the few people with whom he felt totally relaxed. Perhaps, he thought on reflection, she was the *only* person who came into this demanding category. She rarely asked him about work and when she did it was only in vague general terms and never applied any pressure about their personal relationship. They just enjoyed each other's company, savouring the respite from the demands of their jobs. But this evening she seemed reserved, lacking her usual sparkle. The thought crossed his mind that maybe she was having second thoughts about their relationship.

'Everything OK?' he asked in as casual a fashion as possible.

She nodded. 'It's been a bit of a tough week.'

'Oh. You want to talk about it?'

She flashed him a wry smile. 'Shop talk. That's the last thing you want to hear over a quiet drink.'

'Ah, but it's not my shop, so there's no problem. Come on, let's be hearing all about it.'

Matilda took a sip of wine before replying. 'One of our students died last week and it was her funeral today. I went along to represent the school. It was a pretty harrowing experience.'

'I'm sure. How did she die?'

'Well, she drowned. It could have been suicide. It was in the local paper.'

'Oh, I think I know the case. Some of the officers at HQ dealt with it. Not my department. I gather she fell into the canal. Had too much to drink. I didn't realise she was one of your students. I didn't make the connection. What sort of girl was she?'

Matilda shrugged. 'I had very little contact with her. She seemed very ordinary, I suppose. A bit quiet. Average in her studies, I gather. She hadn't really made her stamp on life yet. Now she never will. Just fifteen. What a waste.'

Paul had heard on the grapevine that the case was likely one of suicide. Apparently the girl was pregnant and, he had learned from colleagues, that there was no clue as to who the father was. But he was not about to pass on this information now and depress Matilda further.

'Grim affair, was it?' He asked and regretted it straight away. Any funeral of a fifteen year old was bound to be grim.

'Depressing in the extreme. There were very few mourners: some neighbours, a small group of her school friends, her father and me.'

'No mother?'

'I gather she departed the scene years ago. No one seems to know where she is. The girl lived with her father. He was in quite a state.'

'Understandable.'

Matilda nodded. 'He was howling like a baby through most of the ceremony and there was no one there to comfort him, except the priest. He was particularly caring with the poor soul. One can only guess how one tries to face life after such a tragedy.'

Snow gazed at Matilda, her pretty face shaded with sadness, empathising with this father at the loss of his young daughter. He, who in his profession, was no stranger to tragedy, brutality, violence and sudden loss of life, was hardened to the effects of such personal dramas – he couldn't do his job effectively if he was otherwise – but for Matilda such bleak intrusions, however much on the periphery of her ordered world, must be very upsetting. He reached over the table at took her hand and squeezed it gently. He did not trust himself to say anything in case he plumbed the depths of awful, clumsy platitudes.

The squeeze of his hand brought a softening of the frown on Matilda's forehead and her lips folded into the ghost of a smile.

'I must say,' she said at length, 'events like this do tend to shake my faith a little.'

This was one of many subjects that Snow and she had not touched upon. To him it was a dangerous area for he had strong views which he knew would be at odds with Matilda's. He was an agnostic, cynical and scathing about the idea of there being a benevolent god. Here was a case in point. Why should any omnipotent being with miraculous powers allow this young girl to drown, to lose her young life and that of her child before she had tasted the fruits of existence, fulfilled her potential and, all right, if you insist, atoned for her sins?

Matilda, on the other hand, as headmistress of a Catholic School, was a full convert to that particular doctrine. How staunch a Catholic she was, he could only surmise. They had not discussed religion but Paul reasoned that one does not reach high status in such an institution without being a strong advocate of the Catholic creed. And yet she had never really mentioned her beliefs or feelings on the matter to him and he had certainly kept his lip buttoned on his views.

'That's understandable. There is nothing worse than a child's death,' he said, attempting as neutral a response as possible.

'Suffer the little children to come unto me and forbid them not, for of such is the kingdom of the heavens,' she said softly. 'I suppose poor Mandy has now been allowed entry into the kingdom.'

She and her bastard baby? Not a chance, thought Snow bitterly, while he nodded his head gentle vague agreement. 'How about another drink, eh?' he said.

That night, Matilda Shawcross was unable to sleep. The image of that poor man, Mandy Sullivan's father, kept coming back to her in the darkness. He was ghastly pale, unshaven and unkempt as though he hadn't done anything to himself since he had heard the news of his daughter's death. He could barely stand in church and just hung his head in despair during the two hymns. What added to the tragedy was that there was no one there for him: no friend, close relative, no one to stand by him and hold his hand and whisper words of solace in his ear. He was totally isolated in his grief. His only support was the priest, who comforted him and at times became his physical crutch. After the burial ceremony, Matilda saw the cleric shepherding the man back towards the vestry.

Matilda had not encountered the father before. He had never turned up for parents' evenings and before Mandy's death she had known nothing of the girl's background and this made her feel guilty. As headmistress she should be aware of the lives of all those in her care, especially those in rather difficult circumstances. Obviously a young girl, emotionally vulnerable as she had proved to be, living with alone with her father who had shown little interest

in her education, needed more consideration and attention than the school had given her. And that was her responsibility. Her failing. She was the headmistress after all – the mother superior. With her intervention, closer attention to the girl's situation maybe she wouldn't have ended up …

The thought shocked Matilda and sent an icy ripple down her spine. She turned on her side under the covers and began to pray. To pray for forgiveness and guidance.

CHAPTER TEN

The words of the priest and the manner in which he had treated him after the funeral had helped Frank Sullivan to some extent come to terms with his loss and indirectly his moral transgression; but like a palliative drug, the effect of the priest's words and actions wore off in less than a week and gradually that all-embracing gnawing feeling of despair returned to claim him once more. It seeped into his body, rippling through his veins and stifled his thoughts. He had planned to go back to work on that Monday, but when the day dawned, he could not face the prospect of pretending to return to his old normal life. What was the point? There was no normal life any more. In fact, he had no life at all now. He lay huddled in bed, pulling the bed clothes around him like some magic shield, as though it would protect him from the vicious truths of reality.

And so he lay in bed all day staring at the shifting patterns of light on the ceiling. Sleep avoided him and it was only when he felt the need to go to the lavatory that he managed to pull himself out of the womb-like pit and stumble forth. Once on his feet, he realised that he was hungry and that his mouth was desert dry. Wrapping his old dressing gown around him, he made his way down stairs. He felt creaky and old, his limbs stiff and slow to function after twenty hours or so of inactivity.

He cringed as the fluorescent light sprang into life in the kitchen. The cupboard was virtually bare. There was a packet of teabags and a couple of cans of beans. That would have to do. After putting the kettle on and setting a pan of beans on a low light, he wandered into the lounge and lit the gas fire. He sat huddled up by the flames for a few minutes until he heard the shrill whistle of the kettle. He made the tea and poured out the lukewarm beans on to a plate and returned to the comforting warmth of the fire with them. He spooned the beans into his mouth in a mechanical fashion, hardly tasting the underdone tepid mush. The tea was more satisfying: hot and strong.

He deposited the plate on the tiled hearth and gazed at the congealed orange smear left by the residue of beans. He seemed fascinated by the pattern and reached out with his finger to trace the outer edges of the shiny gloop. Was this it, then? Was this to be his existence, future? Hunched over the fire in his own home, snatching a scratch meal before slinking back up to bed to escape from the world, to escape from himself? He shrugged. Maybe so. He had no energy, no impetus for it to be otherwise. His life was a barren landscape. Well, he mused darkly, perhaps it always was. He tried to think back to a time when he was happy, really happy: when pleasure was relaxed and carefree and not hemmed in by material concerns, various responsibilities, a sense of failure and the feeling that life was always bearing down on him. Running the film of his life backwards at great speed in his mind, he had to reel way back to his childhood for such a moment. It was at Blackpool Pleasure beach. He was… what? Eight or nine? Short trousered and unfettered, he ran in the sunshine through the various stalls and rides, giddy with excitement, entranced by the noise, the garish lights, the joyful cries and screams of girls on the big dipper, the bangs, the screeches, the magical-looking candy floss, the blaring hurdy-gurdy music; all the fun of the fair. It was like a brash kaleidoscope of enchantment. There was that really fat man in the glass case, holding his rotund tummy, swinging backwards and forwards, laughing, laughing, laughing. Laughing fit to bust. He stood before the juddering mechanical figure entranced by and then caught up by its jollity. He started laughing, too. It was contagious. He held his tummy with merriment as tears of joy ran down his young face. He saw that little boy in his mind's eye. He was that little boy. Was this the last time he had been really happy? Happy, with no restraints, no shadows looming in the background. As this vivid scene etched itself on his brain, he realised that he was crying again. But this time they were not tears of pleasure. As he clenched his moist eyes tight he could hear the noises and smell the toffee apples, the candy floss, the hot dogs and the rich ozone aroma of the seaside. And then, suddenly, another sound broke through into his consciousness. It was brighter, sharper, louder. That was because it was real and in the present. It was happening now. His eyes shot open and all the dream-like sensations vanished, shattered like a broken mirror, leaving him with the harsh tring of the doorbell echoing through the silent house.

The sound pierced the darkness with an insistent ferocity. Gradually, he realised what was happening. There was someone at the front door. His front door. It was happening now. Who the hell was calling on him? He never had visitors. Even after Mandy's death had become public, the only people who called were a few neighbours and a chap from work and they had only hovered briefly on the doorstep. The bell rang again followed by a hollow banging on the door. Whoever it was, they were insistent.

Slowly Frank Sullivan pulled himself to his feet and with the stiff movements of an automaton made his way down the hall to the front door.

'I'm coming,' he croaked, in an attempt to silence the banging and ringing, but his voice was feeble from lack of use and had no effect. Turning the knob on the Yale lock, he wrenched the door open to discover a man on the threshold. His features were in shadow.

'Hallo Frank,' the man said. 'I hope I can come in.' He moved forward causing Frank to step back. Confusion filled his mind for a moment and he was just about to ask the man what he wanted when he suddenly felt a violent pain in his stomach. It was fierce and agonising, sending shockwaves throughout his whole body. He cried out in agony and gazing down he saw the man retract the knife from his stomach. The blade was wet with blood. It took him a few moments to realise that it was his blood.

'What… what?' he stammered, his mind in disarray.

The knife pierced his stomach again, the blade moving upwards, slitting the outer flesh.

Frank Sullivan was able to mouth the words, 'Bloody hell' just before his legs gave way and he sank to the floor, his mouth now clapping open and shut with inarticulate groans.

The man leaned over him and continued his task with increased energy. For a few moments his victim squirmed mutely, his eyes wide with pain and terror

But soon it was all over.

Frank Sullivan lay dead in his own hallway.

'We must stop meeting like this. Body-Bags-R–Us, eh?' Chris McKinnon gave a weary half-hearted grin.

Snow was used to the forensic officer's gallows humour. He knew that it was in no way meant to be disrespectful to the corpse which lay at his feet but was simply method of diluting some of the gruesome gravitas of the bleak scenario. A life dealing with dead bodies, many of them mutilated in some manner, could easily eat into your consciousness and wear you down. The only way to fight the enveloping cloud of gloom was to challenge it with humour, flippancy and dubious quips. It provided protection and allowed one to retain a grip on normality.

'Where's your shadow – your trusty DS?'

'Bob. I'm afraid he's succumbed to the flu.'

'Lucky bugger: a day in bed. That's just what I could do with.'

Snow glanced down at the body. 'Who found him?'

'The postman. He was delivering and saw a fair quantity of blood on the doorstep and was suspicious. He looked through the letterbox and saw the body. Nice little surprise.'

Snow gazed down at the bloodied corpse of Frank Sullivan. Despite the number of murdered bodies he had encountered in his career, it still made him feel queasy to gaze at the pallid, blood-streaked skin and features frozen in a twisted agonised grimace of shock or terror. Death came to us all and it was never pleasant but rarely was it as ugly or as gruesome as this.

'What can you tell me?' he said quickly turning to the pathologist.

McKinnon pursed his lips and narrowed his eyes. 'Well, for a start I reckon this is number two. Another little deed carried out by the one who knifed the guy in the street a few weeks ago.'

'Sammy Tindall.'

McKinnon nodded. 'Yeah. Him.'

'What makes you think it's the same murderer?'

'The modus operandi is identical. The cuts are very similar. In fact, I'll stick my neck and say it's a copycat of the last one and I'd bet my pension that it's the same weapon. I'll be able to confirm that when I've carried out the autopsy.'

'Just the news I wasn't waiting for. So now I've got some nutty serial killer to find.'

'It's better that way, isn't? Two murders but only one culprit to apprehend. Two for the price of one.'

Snow smiled grimly. 'You have rather a bizarre way of looking at things – but I suppose you are right. All I have to do now is to try and find some connection between Sammy Tindall and this poor sod in order to give me a lead. Up to now I've got nothing. There must be something that links them.'

'Must there? You were the one who used the phrase 'nutty serial killer'. Aren't they the ones who kill without rhyme or reason? Without a decipherable pattern? Just random slaughter.'

'Thanks for that. Job's comforter you are. Anything else?'

McKinnon gazed down at the corpse and shook his head gently. 'Not at the moment.'

Snow had intended to head back to the office after leaving the crime scene, but instead he made his way to a little café he sometimes frequented which served an excellent double espresso. He reckoned that the potent brew would help stimulate his brain cells or at least provide him with a little warming comfort. Gazing at a bloody dead body did nothing to lift one's spirits. The grey-haired lady in charge gave him a pleasing grin as he entered, a gentle acknowledgement that she recognised him as a past customer. He gave his order and sat at a table by the window. Business was quiet with just three other customers: a pensioner couple and a woman with a bulging shopping bag bearing a supermarket logo. This solitary coffee break was a little bit of luxury. Usually he would have Bob Fellows with him who would keep up a constant stream of chatter hindering Snow from sorting out his thoughts.

The most interesting – if that was the word – aspect of this latest killing was the fact that the victim was the father of the girl who had drowned just over a week before. The girl who had been pregnant. The girl who had been a student at Matilda's school. He could not help thinking that there may be a connection between her death and her father's murder. Added to this there was the mystery of the baby's father. Initially, that had not been important, but now it was. Apparently, there had been no hint of a boyfriend and so it was assumed it had been some reckless casual encounter. A one night stand. The boy probably didn't even know her name or the fact that she was pregnant. That aspect of her death had been kept out of the papers. Whoever he was, he was a link in the insubstantial chain. Maybe an important one. If Snow could discover his identity, it may expose a motive. But of course, there was still the first victim, Sammy Tindall. Where did he fit into the puzzle? What connection – if any - did he have with Frank Sullivan or the girl? It was all very tenuous but one had to begin somewhere.

Snow's coffee arrived, steaming and dark. He savoured it and allowed his thoughts to wander, mapping out in his brain a tentative plan of action.

Mavis Rivers, the school secretary, tapped gently on the Head's door before opening it. 'There's a police officer to see you,' she announced, unable to keep the smirking tone from her voice. 'A Detective Inspector Snow.'

Matilda looked up from her desk in surprise. 'You'd better show him in,' she said after a moment's hesitation. What was this all about, she thought. Strangely, she felt a little flustered. Paul never came to see her at work. They never invaded each other's professional territory, unless…

Snow entered somewhat sheepishly. He, too, felt a little uncomfortable with this scenario. He gave her a brief friendly smile before closing the door behind him. 'Official business, I'm afraid.'

'Oh.' Strangely, she was relieved. She really did not want her boyfriend popping in for an informal visit.

'It's connected with the death of your pupil, Mandy Sullivan.'

Matilda raised her brows in query but said nothing. To Snow she was not quite the same woman he took to the theatre or out for drinks and walks in the park. In her severe black, buttoned up suit, which just allowed the flash of white collar of a blouse at the neck, she seemed rather sexless, nun-like even. Her hair, usually fluffed up and loose was combed sleekly, fitting the contours of her face. She was very much in smooth professional mode.

'I'm afraid her father has been murdered.'

Matilda's eyes widened in surprise and her hand flew to her mouth. 'What! Oh, my goodness, that poor man. Do you know who did it?'

'Not yet. He was killed in his home sometime last night.'

'How terrible. But... why are you here? Why are you telling me?'

Snow pulled a face. 'Mandy. She was pregnant.'

Matilda slumped back in her chair, her features pale with shock. 'Good gracious, you're not pulling your punches today. You never mentioned this before.'

'It wasn't relevant before and I didn't want to upset you.'

'Relevant? How is it relevant now?'

Snow gave a gentle shrug of the shoulder. 'I'm not absolutely sure it is – but I'd like to find out who the father of the child was.'

'You think there may be a connection between him and the murder?'

Snow shrugged. 'It's an avenue worth investigating. I have to follow up any kind of lead.'

'Well, Paul, you won't find the father here. It is a girls' school remember.'

'But you have some male teachers...'

Matilda gasped. 'My God! No. You're not suggesting...'

'I'm playing detective. It's what I do. It wouldn't be the first time a teacher has seduced a pupil.'

'In this school it would.' Matilda's voice had now taken on a brittle tone and her eyes flashed angrily. Paul could sense the defences being erected. 'I trust my staff implicitly. We have no paedophiles here.'

Snow knew that men who preyed on young girls were extremely clever at covering their tracks, providing a highly respectable face to the world. Matilda could easily be mistaken. However, at the moment, he had no real reason to believe that such a creature was involved in this case and as he didn't want to antagonise her any further at this time he changed tack. 'Of course, it may well be that the father is a lad of the girl's own age, someone she met somewhere. It's just important that I find out who he is – if only to eliminate him from our enquiries. That's why I thought if I could have a chat with any friend Mandy had at school that might help. Any close friend with whom she'd share a secret. You know I'd treat it sensitively.'

'I know what you are asking is reasonable, Paul, but it makes me feel very uneasy.' She paused closed her eyes for a moment and then with a sudden brisk movement she stood up and glanced at her watch. 'I didn't know the girl personally so I couldn't tell you about her friends, but her form teacher Ann Sanderson would know. It's nearly lunchtime. I'll check with her and see if she can suggest someone.'

Snow smiled. 'That would be brilliant.'

Matilda did not share the smile. The concept of a senior policeman interviewing one of her girls concerning the sex life of another student was far from 'brilliant' in her eyes.

Debra Scott was a lanky girl who loped in a galumphing round-shouldered way in an effort, Snow assumed, to disguise her height. She had the potential to be pretty but at present, with her straggly unkempt hair, utilitarian heavy tortoiseshell spectacles over which she peered in a somewhat gormless fashion, attractiveness eluded her. By the time she was twenty, thought Snow, she may be turning heads, if only she learned to stand up straight.

Matilda introduced the gentleman to her as 'Inspector Snow' and said that he wanted a little chat with her about Mandy Sullivan. She muttered, 'Poor Mandy,' and glanced at her feet. With some apprehension, Matilda left them alone in her office.

'Mandy and you were good friends, I gather,' said Paul lightly as though he was commenting on the weather.

'I suppose so.'

'You shared interests.'

Debra pursed her lips. 'I suppose so.'

'Like…?'

Debra thought for a moment. 'Some pop music. We like New Kids on the Block. They're cool.'

'What about boyfriends?'

'What boyfriends?'

'Didn't you and Maureen go out with boys?'

Debra sneered. 'No. Course not. Boys weren't interested in us.'

'Why not?'

Debra shrugged her rounded shoulders. 'I suppose because we weren't pretty enough.' She uttered these words simply, in a matter of fact fashion. There was no sense of self-pity in her tone or attitude.

Snow tried to convey the idea that he couldn't really believe this was true with an expression of surprise, but he wasn't sure it was successful. 'The wrong sort of boys then,' he said. Probably it appeared as a patronising leer he thought. 'You never saw Mandy with a boy?' he said.

Debra shook her head. 'Not like that. No.'

'She would have told you if she had.'

'I suppose so.'

'Did you share secrets?'

'Sometimes.'

'What secrets did she share?'

'Just stuff.'

'Mandy had a really dark secret. Did she tell you about it?'

'You mean about her wanting to leave home?'

'Did she?'

Debra nodded and sniffed. 'She didn't get on with her dad. She couldn't wait to finish school and get a job and leave home.'

'In what way didn't she get on with her dad?'

'Not sure really. He liked to sort of control her. She had to do what he wanted all the time. He was possessive like. I suppose it was 'cause his wife had left him. Sometimes he stopped Mandy going out for no reason. He said he wanted her company. He was a bit creepy.'

'Did she confide in you about anything else? Something very serious?'

Snow hesitated. He didn't want to lead the girl and he certainly didn't want her to know the truth if she wasn't already aware of it.

Debra shrugged those shoulders again and looked vaguely puzzled for a moment. 'No,' she said eventually and stared at her feet once more and then as though an idea had suddenly popped into her mind, her face brightened. 'I did sort of feel that that there was something on her mind in the last couple of months or so. She seemed to be... well, a bit miserable all the time. I asked her once if something was up but she said no. We sorted of drifted apart a bit because of it. Didn't see as much of each other as before in the

last few weeks before she... I just got the impression that she just wanted to be alone.'

'And you knew of no reason for this.'

That shrug again. 'Not really – unless her dad was giving her more grief. But she didn't say.'

Snow reckoned they had reached the end of the line on this particular journey. 'Thank you, Debra. You have been a great help. I hope I didn't upset you too much asking you questions about your friend.'

Debra shook her head. 'No. It was nice to mention her again. I miss her. I wish she was still here.' Her eyes moistened behind the heavy spectacles.

There was an awkward silence. Snow really did not know what to say. His experience in dealing with emotional young girls was limited. Debra helped him out by dragging a handkerchief from the pocket of her dress and sniffing loudly. With an awkward movement she turned towards the door. 'Can I go now?' she said.

'Well?' said Matilda returning to her office after seeing Debra loping off down the corridor sniffing on a paper handkerchief.

Snow shook his head. 'Not very fruitful, I'm afraid, but thank you for allowing me to do it.'

'She seemed upset.'

'Yes. Just talking about her friend made her a little tearful. Don't worry, I was gentle and I didn't press her too hard or mention the pregnancy.'

'I'm pleased to hear it. It seems a messy business.' She held up her hand to prevent Snow from responding. 'I am not fishing. Honestly, Paul, I don't want to know the details unless they affect me directly. I have enough on my plate running this school without being party to lurid information concerning a nasty homicide.'

Snow gave her one of his bleak smiles. 'I can assure you, I wasn't going to divulge anything. I still have to be professional about this even though…'

'I am your girlfriend…?'

This time his smile was genuine, accompanied by a chuckle. 'Yes, I suppose you could put it like that.'

She returned the smile, her features and stance relaxing a little. She was glad this interruption in her school life was coming to an end. Impulsively, she leaned forward and kissed Snow gently on the cheek. 'Don't take this the wrong way, but hope I never see you darken the doorstep of my office again in an official capacity. It really is quite disturbing. I would like to keep our official worlds quite separate.'

'I'm with you all the way. I can assure you it was fate rather than personal choice that brought me here. I'll do the best I can not to cause problems. But I do have a serious case to investigate so in the meantime if you'll have a word with some of your staff casually to find out if Mandy was in some kind of relationship with anyone - boy or man.'

She rolled her eyes, her body tensing again. 'And be your mole?'

'No, just make a few casual enquiries, that's all. I assure you I'd ask you to do this even if I didn't know you.'

'I'll believe you, thousands wouldn't.'

There was a policeman on duty standing outside Frank Sullivan's shabby council house when Snow returned. The SOCOs had done their work and vanished but the property would remain a crime scene and under police custody for some time. Snow knew the constable but he flashed his warrant card at him all the same. 'Just come for a little look round,' he explained. The constable nodded and fumbled in his pocket for the key.

Unlocking the door, he held it open for Snow to enter. 'Thank you,' he said.

Stepping into the hall, Snow shivered. It wasn't just the cold that made him do so. There was something icily oppressive about the gloomy atmosphere of the place that seemed to seep under the skin. It was the scene of violence and death and the very fabric of the building seemed to resonate with it. Snow clicked on the electric light but the feeble bulb did nothing to chase away the shadows. There was a dark stain of blood on the hall carpet and the walls were speckled with crimson splashes. The attack must have been sudden and brutal. Either the murderer pushed his victim backwards into the hall or Sullivan had invited him in. Was the killer someone he knew or masquerading as some official? It was very unlikely he would get answers to these questions until the culprit was apprehended. *If* the culprit was apprehended, he corrected himself. There was no guarantee they would catch the bastard. That thought did nothing to lighten his mood.

Casting this depressive notion aside he set about what he came for. To examine the bedrooms of Mandy and Frank Sullivan. The SOCOs had concentrated their efforts on the actual crime scene area where the body had been found. It had been established that the killer had gone no further into the house than the hallway where he had killed his victim before leaving. Therefore the SOCOs had only carried out a perfunctory search on the rest of the premises. Snow was hoping to come across something that would throw more illumination on this confusing case.

The girl's bedroom looked as though it had not been touched since she had been last in it. Probably the father had been too distraught to move anything or tidy it up. It was a common reaction: leave the room as it had been when the victim was alive. It was a typical teenage lair: the wall filled with pictures of pop stars,

The New Kids on the Block featuring prominently, a batch of fluffy toys, the dressing table crammed with make up and jewellery, a portable radio, a cassette player and a rack of tapes. There were some clothes, jeans and dresses hung on the back of the door and across an old wooden chair and a slew of magazines scattered on the bed. The melamine wardrobe that leaned precariously to the left was filled with all kinds of cheap outfits. There was one picture in a plastic frame on the window sill of Mandy herself cuddling a kitten. It had obviously been taken some time ago. She looked about ten and the innocent smiling face that stared out at him, unaware of the dark tragedy waiting to overtake her a few years down the line, gave him a pang of sadness. Sometimes his job brought him too close to the pain and futility of life. It chipped away relentlessly at his sense of decency and hope.

With a determined shrug to slough off such dark thoughts, Snow slipped on his forensic gloves and began his search for personal items. Ideally he hoped to come upon a diary or some photographs which might give him a clue as to who the father of Mandy's unborn child was. He spent half an hour searching the room, crawling under the bed, pulling out all the drawers of the dressing table and examining the contents. There were three handbags stuffed in the bottom of the wardrobe but they provided him with nothing but some bus tickets, a few coins, lipstick stubs and similar innocent paraphernalia. He could find no hidey-hole or secret location where she may have kept a diary or some kind of record of her life. He thought he had found something of significance when he discovered a shoebox wrapped up in a woollen scarf on the top of the wardrobe but it was empty.

With a sigh and a grunt of disappointment, he gave up. If Mandy Sullivan had secrets, she kept them to herself or hid them elsewhere.

He moved along the corridor to the other bedroom. It was a grim chamber which smelt of sweat and staleness. There was an ancient dark wood bedroom suite, probably dating from the forties, consisting of a chest of drawers, a dressing table and a wardrobe and a battered old armchair. The curtains were drawn, although daylight was able to penetrate the thin material. Snow swept them back, flooding the room with illumination which added an even grimmer patina to the room. He began the search. He soon discovered that Sullivan was in possession of a small range of clothes; most, he deduced, were seconds bought off the market. Under a pile of socks in the bedside cabinet he found a tin box which contained fifty pounds in fivers. Beneath the bed was a small suitcase. Despite its location it wasn't dusty, which suggested to Snow that it had not been there long or that it had been used recently.

He hauled it out and plopped it on the bed. To his chagrin he discovered it was locked. What the hell, he thought, and fished out his penknife and attacked the lock. Like so many of Frank Sullivan's possessions, the case was cheap and therefore offered little resistance to his efforts to snap it open. He made quick work of it. With a tight grin of satisfaction, he raised the lid. The case contained a stash of brightly coloured magazines. The titles alone indicated their content, but the lurid pictures on the covers confirmed it. He glanced at two: *Teen Tits* and *Schoolgirl Sex*. A glance was enough. Snow shut the case and sat on the bed.

So that was his unpleasant bag, was it? Snow was instantly reminded of something that Debra Scott had said about Mandy's father: 'He was a bit creepy'. He felt that strange tingle down his spine that he always experienced when he had begun to put two and two together and he didn't like the answer. He really wanted to leave this room. He felt soiled by being in it. It wasn't that it was the decidedly grubby quarters of a murdered man who had a taste for teenage porn. There was something else – something he could not quite put his finger on. He could feel it, appreciate it but could not quite articulate it – not yet at least. Whatever it was, it made him decidedly uneasy. However, such insubstantial notions had to be ignored; he knew he had to press on. There were still a few nooks and crannies to investigate before he could leave. Who knew what else there was yet to discover.

It was in the bedside cabinet, slipped between a pile of underpants. A tatty little diary. It was pink and girly and it did not take Snow very long to determine that it belonged to the daughter rather than the father. He must have taken it from her room at some point – probably after her death. Moving to the window, he read a few pages. It was innocuous stuff: brief comments about lessons, people at school, music she had heard. And then he found a brief entry written all in capital letters: 'HE TOUCHED ME AGAIN TODAY.' There was no further comment just that rather bald but unsettling statement. He flicked through the pages looking for further upper case messages. The next one simply said: 'HAND IN KNICKERS'. And then two weeks later: 'ITS GETTING WORSE. I CANT STOP HIM.' Now the normal girly entries petered out. There were no other comments except the sporadic capital letter notes. And then the one that filled a whole page in large letters; 'GOD HE FUCKED ME TONIGHT.' Snow put down the diary and sighed heavily. So that was it then. Her father. He was the one. He screwed up his face in disgust at the thought. The bastard had groomed his own daughter. Fuelled by his stash of porn magazines, he had sated his appetite on his own flesh and blood; his teenage daughter. The poor kid. Sullivan had obviously discovered the girl's diary after she had died and secreted it in his own room. He couldn't risk it falling into the wrong hands, exposing him for the wretched paedophile he was. Why on earth hadn't he destroyed it? Probably for some perverted sentimental reasons.

Once again Snow was reminded that his job, his profession, his calling as he sometimes thought of it, led him down into the sewers of depravity. Here he was again amongst the shit. He sat on the edge of the bed for some time in this dull, dank room and mentally sifted through his findings, seeing how they fitted in with the facts he already knew. Whether the girl actually committed suicide was still open to question, but, he wondered, had she confided in someone, told someone the terrible truth about her condition and who was responsible for it. And had that someone exacted revenge on Frank Sullivan when the news of Mandy's death became public. It was a viable theory but by no means watertight, especially when one considered Sammy Tindall. Where the hell did he fit into the scenario? As far as could be ascertained Tindall had no connection whatsoever with the Sullivans and yet he was murdered in the same way as Frank Sullivan – a copycat killing, Chris McKinnon had assured him. Surely there couldn't be two of them – a couple of mad killers on the loose - with the similarity between the murders being a bleak coincidence. Snow shook his head as though to dismiss this crazy idea. No, we are not dealing with a lazy TV drama here, this is bloody real life. There must be some link between Frank Sullivan and Sammy Tindall. Some bond however fragile, tentative and hidden. He had no idea what it was but he had to discover it and how poor sad pregnant Mandy fitted into the picture.

Well, he mused, trying to put a positive spin on his cogitations, at least now I have some parts of the puzzle to play about with. He slipped the diary into his coat pocket and with some relief left the room.

It was falling dark as he left the building and the air was stiffening with frost. The constable was still on duty by the door. He gave a brief salute and nod of acknowledgement to his superior officer. Poor bugger, thought Snow, imagining the fellow's boredom and frustration. He was sure he hadn't joined the force to keep watch on a dead man's house in freezing conditions. Slipping into his car, Snow checked the time. It was coming up to five o'clock. It wasn't worth going back to the office now, but he still wanted to follow up a line of enquiry. He decided to grab a quick bite to eat and then make one more call before heading home.

CHAPTER ELEVEN

Matilda slipped off her shoes and sighed. She gazed unseeingly at the document before her on the desk. She had been doing so for at least five minutes. She had a thundering headache and was tired. It had been a trying day. Apart from the mountain of paperwork that the local authority seemed to send her every day, she'd had Paul's visit and its repercussions to deal with. Much as she was fond of him, the intervention of his professional activities into her world was greatly unsettling. She had not enjoyed chatting with the staff in the common room during the lunch hour in a gentle inquisitorial fashion in an attempt to find out details concerning the poor girl who had drowned. It had been a dispiriting experience and had also proved a fruitless one. Despite her efforts, she had discovered there was nothing she could pass on to Paul that would be of any use to him. Mandy Sullivan was a fairly average girl, somewhat dull and not terribly popular, but that was about it. On top of this, in the afternoon she had to deal with an irate parent who was complaining about the lack of progress of her precious child. Apparently it was the incompetence of the members of staff who were not pushing her little darling hard enough, rather than the ability of the girl herself. Matilda had to bring all her diplomatic skills to the fore to deal with this harridan, while exercising remarkable restraint. In truth she wanted to smack the woman across the face and tell the silly cow to go home. It was all very draining and now the school day was over she was ensconced in her office with tedious paper work which she must deal with before leaving. She had to leave her desk clear in readiness for tomorrow's deluge. Matilda heaved a sigh. She felt physically and mentally exhausted and she knew that she was chained to her desk for another hour at least.

She made herself a cup of tea and then returned to the document she had been staring at for some time. She tried once more to bring the print into focus. Half an hour later she had completed that task and was on to the next file. There was a gentle tap on the door and it swung open.

A figure in the doorway waved a cheery greeting. 'The cleaner said she thought it was okay for me to knock and come in.'

The speaker was a tall, good looking man in his late twenties. He had short cropped fair hair, neat regular features and was dressed in a smart blue suit and carried an expensive looking overcoat over his arm. At first his face was in shadow and the light was behind him so that Matilda could not see his face clearly, but she recognised the voice at once. The tone and timbre awakened deep memories. Her body tensed once more.

'Roger...?' she said hesitantly, the word emerging as a question when it should have been a statement.

The man stepped forward into the light.

'Yes, 'tis I,' said the man chuckling, giving a little bow. 'The dark man from your past. You know what they say: bad pennies always turn up, especially when you least expect them.'

CHAPTER TWELVE

The spire of St Joseph's church was beginning to blend with the night sky as Paul Snow emerged from his car. At first glance the gothic Victorian edifice appeared to be all in darkness, but on closer inspection Snow observed a faint flickering glow through the multi-coloured stained glass windows. Briskly he marched up the path and tried the church door. The large ring handle resisted his efforts to turn it at first, but with a determined tug, the old wooden door opened with a recalcitrant creak and he stepped inside.

'Can I help you?' The voice, brusque and edged with suspicion, came from the gloom of the church, beyond the feeble rays of the lantern in the foyer.

Snow turned in its direction and addressed the tall figure glimpsed in the shadows. 'I am a police officer. I wish to speak with Father Vincent.'

A man, dressed in an ancient tweed jacket and baggy corduroy trousers emerged into the dim illumination. He had gnarled exaggerated features, including a bulbous nose and two large goldfish eyes peering out beneath dense, straggly eyebrows.

'You got some identification,' he said taking another step nearer Snow.

'I have,' he said, producing his warrant card and holding it up.

The man scrutinised it carefully for some moments. 'Reckon you're genuine. Got to be careful. We got get a lot of ne'er do wells coming into the church for all sorts of reasons: a night's kip, a swig of communion wine and such. All sorts of reasons.'

'And you are?'

'I am the church warden. I keep everything safe and spick and span. Brian Stead's the name. Nothing goes on in this here church without me knowing it. I can tell you. I say church warden, but I'm part gate keeper too. Stopping all kinds of riff raff coming in here… interfering. I see it as my job to protect Father Vincent from being pestered by all and bloody sundry.'

Not a very Christian attitude, mused Snow, but he kept that thought to himself. He could see from the fierce spark in the man's eyes and the ferocious demeanour that he was not a fellow to argue with.

'Well, I am here on official police business and I'd like to have words with Father Vincent.'

'Mmm,' came the tight-lipped response.

'Where will I find him?'

Brian Stead stared at Snow for some moments, his mouth moving slowly as though he was chewing something unpleasant and deliberating whether to give this policeman the information he required. At length, he spoke. 'He'll be in the vicarage now. That's at the back of the church. Go out the door, turn left, follow the path right round, pass through the graveyard on your right and you'll see the house through the trees.'

Snow nodded. 'Thank you.'

As he turned to go, Stead added, 'Don't keep him too long. He's had a busy day.'

The vicarage turned out to be a modern bungalow. Snow assumed that there must have had been an older building standing in this position, built in the Victorian period at the same time as the church, but for some reason it had been demolished and this modern rabbit hutch erected in its place. It looked as though it had been built sometime in the 1960s. Typical of its period, it was squat, square and utilitarian in appearance; quite ugly in fact.

He made his way up the slippery flagged path and rang the bell. He could hear its modern bing-bong resonate inside. He did not have to wait long before the door opened and the tall cleric stood before him.

'Inspector. Good evening. Do come in. It's too cold to converse on the door step.' Without further conversation Father Vincent led Snow into the shabby brightly lit sitting room. With a hand gesture, Snow was offered a seat.

'Would you care for a cup of tea?

Snow shook his head. 'No thank you, I'm fine.'

'So, what brings you here Inspector? How can I help?'

'Frank Sullivan.'

The priest's features darkened. 'Oh, terrible, terrible. What a tragedy.'

'How well did you know him?'

Father Vincent shrugged. 'Hardly at all'. He smiled faintly and shook his head as though something had amused him. 'We seem to have had this conversation before with regards to Sammy Tindall. As I said then, I get to know my regular parishioners well of course but those who only make, how shall I put it, sporadic visits are generally strangers to me. The fact that they return from time to time pleases me for it seems to show that they are gaining some form of comfort and support from the Lord. I had seen Frank

Sullivan's face in the congregation occasionally but I had not been in conversation with him until the funeral of his daughter.'

'Did he come to confession?'

Father pursed his lips and gave Snow an uncompromising stare. 'You know the situation here, Inspector, surely. I cannot be expected to answer such a question. Whether a man comes to me for confession and what transpires in the Sacrament of Penance remains confidential between the sinner, his priest and God.'

Snow nodded. 'Yes, Father, I am aware of that. I only asked if Frank Sullivan came to you for confession.'

'I still cannot say. The implication in itself would be a betrayal of trust. Such information is within the bounds of my confidentiality.'

'I ask because I think he carried with him the weight of a great sin on his shoulders. One which I believe he would have the need to share, to unburden himself.'

Father Vincent raised his eyebrows in surprise but Snow was not convinced this gesture reflected genuine emotion. 'I see,' said Father Vincent at length.

'You are not curious as to what I'm referring?'

'The man is dead. There is no profit in discussing whatever you consider he did in life. It makes no difference now.'

'Can't you help me here?'

'I am afraid not.'

'Do you know if Frank Sullivan and Sammy Tindall were acquainted with each other?'

A benign smile flittered across Father Vincent's face. 'Oh, dear, you will think that I am deliberately trying to hinder your investigations by my answers, Inspector. But I assure you I am not. My vows as a priest forbid me to discuss any information concerning the Sacrament of Penance and now my ignorance concerning the two gentlemen you have just mentioned leads me

to present you with another negative response. As I've said Mr Sullivan and Mr Tindall were irregular churchgoers and I am not *au fait* with their friendship networks. In simple terms, I have no idea if they knew each other or not. I can say that I never saw them in each other's company in church, but I suspect that is not much of a help.'

'Not really, but then I am chasing errant straws in the wind. Both men have been murdered and all the evidence points to the crimes being committed by the same person...'

'Which prompts you to seek a motive and a connection. I do see. So where does the death of the young girl come into this?'

Snow wondered whether the priest playing with him now? If Frank Sullivan had confessed that he had raped his daughter and fathered her unborn child, Father Vincent would know all about it. If not, well he wasn't about to fill in this gap in his knowledge. Not just yet anyway.

'That's another conundrum I have to solve,' he said.

'I wish you well in your endeavours. May God's help be with you. There are so many wicked people in the world. Let us hope you catch the murderer before he strikes again.'

Amen to that thought Snow.

As he drove away from the vicarage, Paul Snow ran the interview with Father Vincent though in his mind. Despite the priest's intransigence, Snow was convinced that Frank Sullivan had unburdened himself in confessional. If he had not, there really was nothing in the cleric's rules to prevent him from saying so. He wondered, bitterly, how many Hail Mary's Sullivan had been given to absolve himself from the rape of his daughter.

'I was hoping you could put me up for a few weeks, till I get a place of my own.'

'You intend to stay around here?' Matilda could not keep the note of surprise and dismay from her voice.

'Why not? I'm a free agent – now. Be close to my big sister. We can get to know each other again.'

Matilda was tempted to respond with, 'I know you too well already', but she bit her tongue instead.

She and her brother Roger were back at her house and he was lounging on the sofa while she stood uneasily in front of the fireplace.

Suddenly, he leaned forward, his features concerned and serious. 'Look Mat, there's no need to worry. I have changed, you know. Really, I have. I've paid my dues for running off the rails. I'm a good boy now and I intend to stay that way but I do need a little help, some encouragement to get me started again.'

Matilda forced a smile. 'Of course. Your sudden appearance has taken me by surprise that's all. You can stay in the spare room for a few weeks while you get yourself sorted.' The words made her mouth dry. It was the last thing she really wanted to say. She had an overwhelming sense that her fairly placid, organised life was about to go into freefall.

'That's great,' Roger grinned, his serious mask evaporating as easily as it had appeared. 'Now then, what does a man have to do to get a drink around here? I'm gagging for a gin and tonic.'

CHAPTER THIRTEEN

Snow had not seen Matilda since his visit to her school. It had bothered him that his professional life had intruded upon hers. He was aware how discomforting she had found it and he too had felt awkward dealing in a formalised way with someone he was close to. He felt somehow that the experience had sullied their relationship a little. It was as though this rather brittle encounter had placed a barrier between them. He thought that it was significant that she had not been in touch with him since, not given him a ring for a chat or arranged a date. Certainly they didn't live in each other's pockets and the demands of their jobs often meant they did not see each other for days, even a week, but there was always the odd phone call, usually late at night, to help bridge these gaps. But not now. However, he was well aware that he had not contacted her either and now as Friday dawned he was feeling guilty about it. While in the shower that morning, he decided to break this impasse. He couldn't live his life with these uncertainties. It was time to call her and arrange for a meeting that evening if she was free. At least then he would know where he stood.

He towelled himself dry and while still in his robe, he padded downstairs and reached for the phone. He knew that she left for school early, but at this time he reckoned that he would catch her before she set off. As he dialled the number, suddenly he felt a warm glow of affection for Matilda. Despite his uncertainties about their relationship, he really was fond of her and felt very comfortable in her company. It would be a great shame if something happened to spoil that. The phone rang for some time and his spirits sank as he thought he must have missed her. Then his call was answered.

'Hello,' said a voice. It sounded cross and harsh. It was a man's voice.

For a few seconds Paul was perplexed. Have I misdialled, he thought, and got the wrong number.

'Hello,' the voice said again.

'I was hoping to speak to Matilda Shawcross.'

'You've missed her. She's gone to work already.'

It wasn't the wrong number then.

'Thanks,' he said hesitantly.

Abruptly, the receiver was replaced at the other end and his ear filled with a sharp burring sound.

Well that was a bolt from the blue. He wandered into the kitchen somewhat in a daze and made himself a strong coffee. 'What was that all about?' he murmured and then took a sip of scalding coffee, allowing it to burn the inside of his mouth and taking some perverse pleasure from the process. Come on, he chivvied himself, you are the detective: explain that scenario. Who was that answering the phone in Matilda's house – after she had gone to work? Too early for a workman/repairman - surely. Paul knew of no other men in Matilda's life – at least none that she had told him about. There had been the husband but he was long gone and not likely to return. The voice was brisk and alert, suggesting youth rather than age. Was it time for alarm bells to start ringing? Surely, it couldn't be another boyfriend? She was not the type to two time him – or anyone. It was not in her nature. Or had he been fooled? Well, it wouldn't be the first time. These thoughts niggled at him as he drained the coffee mug and got dressed.

If he, Paul Snow, had one sterling trait, it was his ability to be patient – an ideal quality for a policeman. He would now have to exercise this regarding Matilda. He couldn't rush at the problem in a clumsy and aggressive manner. He would have to wait and see how things fell out.

As he pulled up in the car park at the Huddersfield HQ, he compartmentalised this nagging dilemma, pushing it the back of his mind and attempted to focus on the demands of his job. A snotty, sniffing Bob Fellows was waiting for him in his office. He had returned to work the day before but still looked like death warmed up. The rheumy eyes and red nose indicated clearly that the heavy cold was still in residence.

'I've had a thought,' he said as Snow hung up his coat.

'How did it make its way through the mucus?'

'Slowly with wellington boots on.'

Both men smiled.

'Go on, dazzle me with your thought. I really need stimulating this morning.'

'The Tindall and Sullivan case. Perhaps we are dealing with an ancient grudge here.'

'Go on, Sherlock.'

'Well, there seems little to connect these two men...'

'For little read 'nothing'.

'Yes,' agreed Bob, dabbing his nose with his handkerchief. 'Apparently they didn't know each other. They didn't mix in the same social circles. In fact they didn't seem to have any social circles.'

'Which is indicative of something, I suppose.'

'That they were a pair of miserable buggers.'

'You put it so elegantly and succinctly.'

'But that might not have always been the case. What if they'd known each other say ten or maybe twenty years ago – when they were young men. They live in the same town and were about the same age. It's not beyond the bounds of possibility that they had known each other then: worked for same firm maybe, played on the same team, hung out in the same boozer or courted the same girl even. Something that links the two of them and, indeed, links them to the next victim.'

'Don't say that!' groaned Snow. "Next victim', indeed.' He rubbed his chin and thought for a moment. 'You could have a point. It's certainly worth digging back into their histories to see what we can come up with. School days, work patterns, clubs etc. Good thinking, Batman. At the moment it seems to be the only straw that we can clutch at. Okay, off you go, take your snotty carcass out of here and follow that up. Let me know if find out anything significant.'

Bob Fellows gave a mock salute and sniffed noisily before leaving the room.

Snow made himself a coffee: a thick black brew which was his drug. He had never counted how many mugs of the stuff he downed in a day, perhaps because he was aware that if he did he would be appalled at the number. He sat at his desk and sighed as he gazed at the two files sitting there. He knew he had to sift through the material yet again to see if there was anything, anything at all, that might give him some kind of lead in the Tindall and Sullivan murders. He also knew that this would be a fruitless task.

Half an hour later, he felt his eyelids drooping and the text misting before him. He had read it all before, scrutinised it before and analysed it before. There was nothing new. Nothing tangible to grasp and run with. Suddenly he thought of Matilda

and the phone call earlier that morning. Initially, he was annoyed for allowing thoughts of a personal matter intrude while he was working but he justified this intrusion to himself by realising that here at least was a mystery he could clear up quite easily. With one telephone call.

He gazed at the phone on his desk. It stood there in its shiny black case beckoning to him. He glanced at his watch. 9.30. School assembly would be over. Probably Matilda would be in her office now. Well, he could find out. He snatched up the receiver and rang the school. He got through quite quickly to the secretary. 'I'll see if Miss Shawcross is free,' she said calmly and efficiently.

Paul waited and began to wonder if he had done the right thing. Had he been too impulsive? He heard the receiver being lifted at the other end. It was too late now.

'Hello.' The tone was neutral, if anything, apprehensive.

'Hello Matilda. Sorry to bother you at work.'

'Is it about the Sullivan girl?' The voice was laden with concern.

'No, no. It's... well it's a personal matter. I rang you at home this morning, wondering if you'd like to meet up for a drink this evening...'

'Really. I didn't get the call.' Her voice seemed strained, distant.

'No. You'd gone to work. A man told me.'

'Ah.'

He waited a moment but she said no more and so he jumped in, feet first. 'I was wondering who he was.'

'I have a house guest at the moment. I'll tell you about him later.'

Why not now? A simple explanation was all that was needed. Wasn't it?

'It's complicated,' she added.

What the hell did that mean?

'Well... I was wondering... how about that drink this evening?'

'I'm sorry but I've got rather too much on at present. I'd love to… but I can't. Can we leave it for now?'

Leave it for now! Was he getting the heave ho? Certainly sounded like it.

'Sure, anything you say.'

'Call me next week, eh? At work.'

Not at home. Not where 'the house guest' is.

'Yes, sure. Bye for now then.'

'Yes, bye.'

He lowered the receiver and stared ahead, his forehead frozen in a frown. He had been wrong. He had given up on one mystery in the belief that he would solve a less puzzling one. But now he was more confused than before. Matilda was behaving oddly. For some reason she didn't want to see him – not for the moment at least - and there was a man living in her house. Perhaps it was the beginning of the end which perhaps, he mused reluctantly, was for the best given his own deep rooted uncertainty about the future of such a liaison. He was well aware that his own innate sexuality had not been eradicated, conquered or whatever phrase he could think of to suggest that it had gone away. It was, he knew, only sleeping. Matilda was not a cure. And yet she had given him comfort, warmth and affection which he had not experienced in his adult life before. That he would miss and the thought of life without her saddened him greatly.

Suddenly, he realised that his fists were clenched, the nails digging into the flesh of his palms. He gave a snort of irritation. He was over-reacting, growing melodramatic, creating a bleak scenario from a few minor uncertainties. However, he knew that he would not be at ease until found out what was really going on.

CHAPTER FOURTEEN

He knew that this one had to be different – if only to buy him some more time. He had already set a kind of pattern and he was aware that the police would be desperately trying to fathom it out. He didn't underestimate their intelligence, aware that a third victim with similar provenance would be helping them too much. Guiding them towards the truth. Leading them to him. That must not happen. He had no desire to help them at all. He knew, of course, that he would be caught in time. He was philosophical about that, but he wanted to carry on a lot longer than this. Two was a minor number. There had to be more: the body count had to be much bigger before the end came. So now it was time to throw a spanner in their works and confuse the issue for the gentlemen of the law. The notion pleased him and warmed his soul.

He sat at the kitchen table and spread out the local newspaper and gazed at the article on page four, in particular at the grinning features of a swarthy fellow who with charmless aplomb was sticking two fingers up at the photographer. This was Simon Barraclough caught outside Hull Prison on his recent release. As the article revealed he had served his two year sentence for aggravated burglary and was once more a free man. His leering features quite clearly indicated that two years in choky had not chastened him one jot. There was no remorse or shame imprinted on those grim features – only gloating defiance and brutish arrogance. The two-fingered gesture epitomised the nature of the beast. His expression told it all: 'I've got away with it. Two years at Her Majesty's pleasure was a doddle, so fuck you'.

Indeed, as the article reported, there had been an outcry at the time Barraclough was convicted. It had seemed to many that it was a ludicrously light sentence for the crime. He had broken into the home of an eighty-five year old woman, a Mrs Ivy Spencer, terrorised her and stolen cash and ornaments. Within hours of the robbery, Mrs Spencer had collapsed. She died the following day of a heart attack brought on by the trauma of the robbery. Mrs Spencer's daughter claimed that Barraclough had effectively murdered her mother and this was the main thrust of the case for the prosecution. However, Barraclough had no previous convictions and appeared convincingly contrite and emotionally upset in the witness box that the judge apparently fell for his bluster and play acting. And so he was given just a three years custodial sentence and was out in two. Out and grinning. It was not right, thought the man staring at the newspaper article. Indeed it was very wrong. It was a wrong he intended to correct. He ran his forefinger over the newspaper, circling the face of Simon Barraclough and drawing a sharp line across his neck. That smile, he thought, that demon smile, would soon become a rictus death grin.

Matilda Shawcross pulled into her driveway and brought her car to a halt. She saw all the lights blazing in her house and felt the knot tighten in her stomach. She had always regarded her home as a kind of womb-like haven, a place where she could escape the stress and pressures of her job. This was her domain where she could do what she liked and there were no rules only her own wishes and desires. Running a school was rewarding and sometimes exciting and fulfilling but it certainly was not easy. The demands made upon a head teacher were growing by the day and more and more she needed the solace, privacy and comfort that her home offered. She could close the door on that part of her life and become herself, become Matilda instead of Miss Shawcross for a time at least.

But not now.

With the arrival of Roger back in her life and in her home, there were other pressures and concerns to nag at her. Her personal space had been invaded in such a casual, brutish way and she had been surprised how much it had affected her. Roger had been there less than a week and yet already her tidy, well-ordered house was in a state of disarray. There was mess everywhere. It seemed that he was incapable of closing a drawer, making a cup of coffee without leaving some kind of detritus, filling ashtrays without emptying them and possessed a pathological inability to turn any light off. And then there was his physical presence. He seemed to be everywhere: she had no private spaces left.

However, what was worse, and what seemed to be preying in her mind all her waking hours, was how long this was going to last. Despite his words of assurance he appeared to have done nothing to seek alternative accommodation or find himself employment. He seemed content to hang around the house most of the day, watching television and drinking gin and then disappearing for some time in the evening, returning well after midnight. My God, it was like living with an errant teenager. She knew that they would have to have that talk soon. That talk that she had scripted in her head but had not as yet mustered up sufficient courage to instigate. She wanted her house back and her life. And she wanted him gone. The longer he stayed the longer the situation became the status quo – and that was not going to happen.

She slammed the car door, gritted her teeth as she saw all the windows ablaze. As she approached her own front door with apprehension a sudden spark of anger ignited within her. Why on earth should she feel this way about entering her own house? This was ridiculous. However, as she turned the handle of the door she couldn't help wishing that she had called in at some bar on the way home for a drink to buoy up her courage. She was used to confrontation at work but not in her personal life – not since her divorce at least.

She entered the hall and heard music playing in the sitting room. Dropping her briefcase down and hanging up her coat she made her way there. A young man who she had never seen before was sitting in a relaxed pose on the sofa, smoking a cigarette. He raised his head casually as she entered and smiled.

'Oh, hi,' he said dreamily. He was good looking with an affected casualness of dress. He wore a light coloured grey suit with a collar and tie, but the knot was slack and the top button of the shirt was unfastened. His blonde hair flopped about his face in a Byronic fashion. He was completely unfazed by her appearance in the room.

'And who are you?' Matilda asked, only just managing to keep her fury in check.

'That's Mark.' It was Roger who replied. He appeared from the kitchen carrying a drink, the ice cubes clinking noisily in the glass. 'He was just going, weren't you, Mark?'

The young man turned to look at Roger, an expression of surprise on his face. 'Er, yes,' he said at length. 'I guess I was.' He rose awkwardly from the sofa and adjusted his tie.

'You can see yourself out, can't you, Mark?' Roger said pointedly, before taking a sip from the glass.

Mark opened his mouth as though he was about to say

something but then thought better of it. Instead he nodded mutely and made his way swiftly towards the door, averting his gaze from Matilda. A few seconds later there was the sound of the front door opening and closing.

Roger shrugged and gave his sister a weary smile. 'Old habits…' he said before sipping his gin and tonic.

Later that night, Matilda lay in bed, staring at the ceiling. She was unable to sleep: her body was tense and her mind racing with thoughts. How could one man's return into her life cause her so much anguish? Within a remarkably short time Roger had disturbed the comparatively quiet waters of her life. But then he had always been trouble. He was five years younger than her and when he had been a very young child she had enjoyed mothering him, playing the older, wiser sibling and he had responded to her care and affection. She had been a junior school teacher even in those days. It had been a happy relationship, but when he had reached puberty, his character changed and darkened. He sought dominance and this came through mischief and any activity that challenged the norm. He was forever getting into trouble at school and his first brush with the law came when he was just fourteen. He had threatened a master at school with a knife and the police had been called in. This action, thought Matilda, was typical of Roger: it was violent, aggressive and foolish. He had given no thought to the upset his behaviour would cause to either himself or his family. He never did. He either never considered the consequences of his actions or he ignored them.

Matilda's father had died when Roger was eleven and so there was no strong male influence in the house to help shape and control this difficult teenager who seemed determined to live a life off the rails. Matilda's mother was a gentle soul and was a not able to rein in the extravagant and delinquent behaviour of her son. Matilda saw that she gradually gave up trying. And then, just after he turned sixteen, Roger came to the conclusion that he was gay. Far from confusing or upsetting him, he welcomed this revelation with open arms. It further established his difference from the main stream of society which pleased him greatly. Convention was not for him.

His school career had been fairly horrendous but he was talented in English and showed much promise as a writer. On leaving school, he eventually managed to get a job on a local paper down south. He packed his bags and disappeared from the lives of Matilda and her mother. They only had the odd letter and phone call, and one Christmas, a visit from Roger. It had been a bleak festive occasion but Roger assured them that he was working his way up the journalistic ladder and was sure that before he was twenty five he would have a job on a London paper or magazine. But his wayward sex life had led him into the world of drugs. From being a user he had progressed into drug dealing which eventually landed him in gaol with a stiff five year sentence. By this time their mother had died and when Matilda had gone to see him in gaol, he had refused to see her. He later wrote to her stating that he did not want to be reminded of his previous life and she must not feel any obligations to visit him. And so, in effect the link was broken. It did not affect Matilda too much. In essence, the rift had occurred many years before and now she was relieved to be cut adrift from such a disruptive force. But blood will out, she supposed, and she did find herself from time to time wondering how Roger was. But gradually these thoughts had faded. She had made a pleasant but demanding life for herself without any reference to her renegade brother. She never mentioned him to anyone. She had edited him out of her life.

Until now.

Strong in the knowledge that sleep was not an option for the time being, she sat up in bed, pulling the pillows up behind her back to support her in a sitting position and took a sip of water from the glass on her bedside cabinet. She thought back to the previous evening. They had had the talk that she planned. After a fashion.

What really angered and frustrated Matilda was that Roger seemed oblivious of his faults. He reacted to her complaints and concerns with an easy grin and a gentle shrug of the shoulders. It was his standard reaction to censure. She remembered those movements from his youth, the curl of the lips, the air of bewilderment registered in those light blue eyes. Part of it, she knew was an act, but also part of it was Roger's innate inability to take responsibility for his own actions. He just didn't care.

After she had exhausted her ire, he apologised if he had upset her and assured her that he would move out 'within the fortnight'. He also promised that he would not bring any more of his boyfriends around to the house again. And then he had leaned forward and kissed her on the cheek. 'Sorry for being a nuisance, Sis. Forgive me. I'm still finding my feet after being... away for some time.'

She knew it was a performance but she was grateful that hadn't exploded with indignation, which was another of his traits. For the moment she had to take him at his word. What else could she do? He was, after all, her brother.

Matilda took another sip of water and sighed.

CHAPTER FIFTEEN

The unleashed Fox Terrier raced towards Paul Snow, its whole body electrified with excitement. It made to jump up at him, but Snow leaned forward and held out both hands to gently ward off the dog. He didn't want the creature's muddy paws staining his cord jeans.

'Woody, get down,' came the cry from one of the dog's owners, an anoraked couple in their fifties, who were hurrying down the path towards him. The man looked like a bank manager and the woman one of those Conservative ladies who hold lunches at home to raise money for the starving in Africa. The man grabbed the dog with both hands and pulled him away from Paul and snapped on his lead. 'Sorry about that. He's easily excited,' he said smoothly.

Paul smiled. 'That's OK. He certainly is a lively fellow isn't he?'

'You wouldn't think he was nearly nine years old, would you?'

Paul increased his smile. 'No, I wouldn't.'

'Well, come on old chap, let's be off,' said the man, addressing the dog. With an exchange of amiable nods the couple moved on.

It was the first human interaction he'd had in nearly twenty four hours. It was rare for Paul to have a full weekend off from his duties and, unlike most people, he did not really relish them. With no family or close network of friends, he tended to spend them alone. Recently his relationship with Matilda had changed all that. They usually spent at least one of the two days together: a walk, a pub lunch, a visit to a museum, art gallery and the occasional movie. He had experienced the nearest he had ever come to a sort of normal domestic existence in his grown up life. But now that was put on hold. Maybe it was over for ever. That thought made him sad. He still had great difficulty thinking of Matilda in a full romantic way, but he was glad of her company and was very fond of her. It also delighted him to know that she was fond of him too. Maybe that notion should be phrased in the past tense now.

He had been tempted to ring her on the Saturday but he had decided not to. She had said that she would get in touch with him when she was ready and he had to stick by that. He didn't want aggravate the situation further by appearing too inquisitive or needy. As a detective, he was frustrated and disappointed at not being able to come up with some theory or reason why she should be acting like this and, more pertinently, who that man was who had answered her phone. He would simply have to employ that stoical patience which was his stock in trade as a professional policeman.

Sunday had dawned bright and crisp and he decided he needed fresh air and a change of scene. He had driven over to Bolton Abbey and taken the path over by the Strid. It was still too early for many walkers and he'd had the place to himself apart from a few red-faced determined joggers, until he had encountered Woody, the over enthusiastic terrier, and his owners. But they, too soon disappeared from the landscape and he was alone once more. This thought struck him philosophically. He did lead a solitary life. It wasn't just his sexuality and his desire to contain that and keep it secret that led him down this particular avenue. It was part of his nature, too. He was aware that he was most comfortable, more himself, when he was on his own. He was conscious that in company, whether with colleagues or others, even including Matilda, there was always an element of performance in his behaviour. 'Putting on a show' as his mother would have said. There was little he could do about it now. He lacked the talent to be simply sociable. That gene was missing from his makeup and so he mainly settled for his own company. In his mid-thirties it had become his way of life. As he mulled these thoughts over, he came to accept that it would probably be best if his relationship with Matilda faltered and came to an end. At one point, he suspected that she was hoping for a long term thing, maybe even marriage. But that would be unfair on her... well, on both of them. He was very doubtful that he could commit fully, in the emotional sense, to such an arrangement and as such, it would be a dark betrayal to Matilda who deserved better.

This thought lay heavily on his mind as he broke through the shady wooded section of the walk and made his way down the path towards the river, its waters glinting brightly in the late autumn sunshine. He passed a quartet of cheery walkers who all nodded at him and gave the customary countryside greeting of 'Morning' and strangely this civilised custom raised his spirits. He spied the Cavendish Pavilion café further down on the other side of the river with the smoke rising lazily from its chimney and the thought of a cup of coffee and a flapjack gave him a shiver of pleasure. He increased his pace in anticipation of the treat. He determined that, for the time being, he would cast all serious and muddled thoughts aside. He had come out to unwind a little and that would not happen if he mulled over matters that concerned either his private or professional life. Reality was waiting in the wings and would intrude all too soon.

He gazed up at the pale blue sky, flecked with a few ragged clouds and for some reason he smiled and broke into a jog. He could almost taste that flapjack already.

CHAPTER SIXTEEN

The bedsit that the authorities had found for Simon Barraclough was basic in the extreme. 'If I had a fuckin' cat,' he had moaned to a mate, 'I wouldn't be able to swing the bastard round.' At first he had vowed to move out of this shithole as soon as he could, but as he melded back into civilian life after two years of being banged up – one with easy-going mates, cheap beer and real street-walking freedom - the restrictions of his new living quarters did not seem so important. After all they were better than his cell and he didn't have to share his space with a smelly halfwit or piss into a bucket.

His complaints to his probation officer about the bedsit faded, and he spent most of his energy finding excuses not to go for job interviews. He was happy with the dole for the time being. It brought him sufficient cash to allow him to get rat-arsed when he wanted and the freedom to laze around in bed all day if he wished. Should he start to fall short of cash he could always go on the thieving again.

What he really wanted now was a girlfriend. Correction. What he really wanted now was a girl he could shag. Several years of satisfying himself had built up his appetite for the real thing. He had a strong aversion to paying for sex. That was a desperate measure but needs must sometimes.

She was young and no doubt a druggie. She could be barely out of her teens but with all that make-up plastered all over her face it was difficult to tell. She was slim though. He liked them like that: lean and childlike. He couldn't understand these men who lusted after big tits and fat arses. No, this one, this Gwen, that's what she called herself, would do. He picked her up in The Shoehorn bar in town. It was easy peasy. It was clear she was desperate for cash and not too fussy. She was already groggy with drugs when he got her back to his place. He just hoped that she wasn't going to pass out on him in the heat of the action.

He manoeuvred her down the narrow passage which led from the door to the space where he lived. It was an untidy shambles with the main items of furniture being a dead sofa and a narrow bed.

'You gotta drink,' she said, sitting down on the bed. 'My mouth's really dry.'

'What d'you think this is? A fuckin' cocktail bar?' Despite his annoyance, he grinned at his own allusion.

The girl pulled a face. 'You're a charmer, aren't you?'

'Listen, darlin', I'm paying you for a shag not to play house. So get your kit off.'

The girl's body stiffened and her features darkened. She half rose from the bed. She had good mind to leave this creep now. And then the thought of stepping out into the cold again and trawling the streets for business made her pause and with some reluctance she sat back down on the bed. 'Well, I'd like to see the colour of your money before we start.'

Barraclough reached into the back pocket of his jeans and extracted his wallet. 'We said forty…'

'It was fifty. I need fifty.' There was such a desperate wail in her voice that it prompted Barraclough not to argue. 'Have it your own way,' he growled and, extracting the money from the wallet, cast the notes on the bed. The girl quickly scooped them up and stuffed them in her purse.

'Right,' he said, 'now get your kit off.'

The girl stood up and without embarrassment threw off her thin outer coat and then slipped the mini-dress over her head until she stood, head bowed, in her bra and knickers, her pale skin already dappled with goose pimples. Barraclough unbuckled his jeans and slipped them off. She could see from the bulge in his underpants that he already had an erection. He moved forward and pushed her gently down on to the bed. His rough hands were soon tugging at her knickers.

'Careful,' she said. 'Don't rip 'em.'

'Shut up,' he said, yanking the knickers down her legs and flinging them across the room.

In her grim profession, Gwen had experienced many men who had seen her not so much as a human being, not even a nameless sex object, but just as a piece of meat to be penetrated with as much force, and it would seem, as much anger as possible. Simon Barraclough was one of the worst of this breed. With his eyes bulging like a wild animal, he thrust himself into her with a kind of determined mechanical rhythm that lacked any shred of humanity or passion. It was more an act of brutal dominance. He was taking out his pent up frustration with life on her frail body. He was not indulging in an act of pleasure but one of punishment. For the girl it was both painful and demeaning, but she had grown used to both. In the time honoured tradition of the whore, she laid back and, rather than think of England, she allowed her thoughts to dwell on the fifty pounds waiting for her when this degrading ordeal was over. The fifty pounds and what it would buy her: a brief escape from this dunghill that was her life.

As is the case with men like Barraclough, he was unable to sustain prolonged intercourse. His fury and vigour won over any sense of maintaining the act. It was concluded in less than two minutes. With the roar that a rampant bull would have been proud of, he climaxed and with a grunt, slipped sideways on the bed, panting gently, his brow dripping with sweat.

Gwen lay still. She knew from experience that it was not her place to suggest that the transaction was over. She prayed that he wouldn't attempt a second assault but she had to wait a few minutes in case he did. Eventually, he sat up and retrieved his underpants and jeans from the floor. She gave a silent sigh of relief. She waited until he had zipped up his pants before reaching for her dress.

Suddenly there was a violent banging on the door. It thundered in the room.

'What the fuck!' exclaimed Barraclough. He made a move towards the door and he did so the noise stopped as suddenly as it began.

Barraclough's features clouded with puzzlement. He now seemed uncertain what to do.

And then the noise came again: a rapid loud banging. The door shook with the force of it.

This time Barraclough strode down the narrow passage, his hands clenched and his eyes blazing. 'What the fuck,' he snarled again and pulled open the door. Standing before him was a tall shadowy figure who took a step over the threshold.

'What the...' Barraclough began his mantra once more, but then his attention was captured by the sudden pain in his abdomen. His mouth gaped open in silent shock. It felt as if someone had set fire to his intestines. As he staggered backwards, he gazed down and saw the handle of the knife that had been thrust into his stomach. The dark figure thrust deeper and then grasping the handle dragged the blade upwards, tearing his flesh and slicing through his innards.

Gwen had been concentrating on retrieving her knickers when she heard Barraclough emit a strangulated cry and as she glanced down the corridor she saw him slump to the floor. Standing over him was the dark figure of a man holding a knife. The blade flickered briefly in the dim light and she saw that it was stained with a dark substance. She clamped her hand over her mouth to stifle the whimper of shock which was about to emerge. With great alacrity, she dropped into a crouching position and dodged back out of the dark man's line of sight. Gwen wasn't quite sure what was happening or whether the man with the knife had seen her but she knew she was frightened and sensed great danger. She did not know whether Barraclough was dead or not, but it was clear that he had been attacked by the intruder. She scuttled to the corner of the room, sank to her knees down at the far side of the bed and held her breath. There was a muffled silence. In her frightened state, it felt as though time had stood still. And then she heard the door slam shut.

Still she waited, shivering with dread, still not daring to move. Was the man now making his way down the corridor, his knife in his hand? Was he coming to kill her? This terrible though made her cry out and she bit her knuckle in an attempt to muffle the noise. Frozen by fear to the spot, she waited for whatever terrible fate awaited her.

But nothing happened.

There was no further noise and no one appeared around the corner from the passageway. Had he gone – or was he just waiting to pounce? After a long time, she got to her feet and like a timid child made her way towards the corridor and tentatively peered around the corner.

There was no one there. No one, apart from Simon Barraclough who was lying, slumped sideways against the wall. He was not moving.

'Oh, my God, my God,' Gwen whispered, her whole body shaking, as she moved slowly down to corridor towards the prone shape.

It did not take her long to realise that her customer of the evening was dead. The front of his body, around the abdomen, was running with blood, glistening like dark slime in the dim light. It had flowed through his clothing and was now dripping down onto the threadbare carpet. She retched at the sight and turned away, tears springing to her eyes. It was a nightmare. Was this real or were the drugs playing tricks with her brain? She stumbled back to the bed and curled up into a foetal position, sobbing uncontrollably.

Not far away, out in a nearby darkened street, the murderer was moving swiftly towards his car, satisfied with the night's events, feeling that he had, to use the phrase, killed two birds with one stone. He smiled at the concept. Yes, indeed, he had managed to muddy the waters for the police – or so he believed – and had continued his crusade most successfully.

CHAPTER SEVENTEEN

It was nearly midnight when Snow and Bob Fellows arrived at the large Victorian house situated on New North Road, just a mile from the centre of Huddersfield. It was a hive of police activity, with a couple of flashing patrol cars and a number of officers milling around the main entrance. Despite the late hour a small crowd of curious onlookers had gathered on the pavement on the opposite side of the road. Entering the building, Detective Sergeant Martyn Cripps greeted Snow with a laconic nod and led them up to Simon Barraclough's bedsit.

'There is a witness – of sorts. A girl.'

'Oh.'

'Yes, a tart. She'd had sex with the victim just before the attack. He picked her up earlier in the evening.'

'So she witnessed the murder.'

'She's a bit vague as to details. Don't count on her for much. I reckon she'll be about as useful as a chocolate teapot,' said Cripps sourly.

'Why's that?'

'She's a druggie and claims she didn't see anything clearly – no doubt the pink rabbits and multi-coloured bubbles blurred her view. You know what these types are like. You can't rely on anything they say. Their brain's in cloud cuckoo land. She's down at the station now.'

'Just our luck,' said Bob.

Snow did not comment. They passed through a group of SOCOs in the corridor and reached the entrance of the bedsit. Chris McKinnon was standing over the body and grinned ghoulishly at their approach. 'Not a pretty sight.'

Snow had to agree as he gazed down at the crimson-stained creature lying in the hallway, the vicious wounds clearly visible through the torn clothing and dried blood. The stomach had been savagely ripped open, exposing some of the corpse's innards. Snow grimaced and averted his gaze

'In my humble opinion,' McKinnon was saying, 'this is your number three. Same method of attack as Sammy Tindall and Frank Sullivan. Sharp, serrated knife thrust into the abdomen, a full frontal attack, and then sliced upwards. Not terribly scientific but extremely effective.'

Snow looked down once more at the mutilated corpse. 'Who is he?'

'That's Simon Barraclough, bastard of this parish,' announced Martyn Cripps, moving into the circle standing by the body. 'Local bad boy. Just out of the nick. A ne'er do well if there ever was one. There'll not be many who will mourn his passing'.

'So what happened here?' asked Bob Fellows, bending down to examine the body. 'It looks like he answered the door and was stabbed for his pains?'

'That's how I read it,' said McKinnon.

'Just like Frank Sullivan,' observed Snow

'Indeed. There's no sign of a struggle. It must have been swift and sudden.' McKinnon mimed the action of the attack. 'The poor bastard didn't have a chance.'

'Hardly a poor bastard,' sneered Cripps.

'So the killer stabbed him and just left,' said Snow, thinking aloud.

'Yes. Apparently the girl hid out of sight. Round the corner,' said Cripps pointing the way.

'Let me see.'

Stepping carefully over the corpse, Snow moved down the corridor into the main area of the bed sit. He gazed around, making a mental note of the layout and then returned to the doorway.

'Come on, Bob. I think we're done here. Let's see what this girl can tell us.'

Gwen was sitting in a cell back at the police HQ, a blanket draped over her shoulders, staring down at the mug of hot milky coffee cradled in her hands.

'How are you feeling?' asked Snow gently as he pulled up a chair and sat opposite her.

'Like shit,' she said sourly, not looking up.

'You'll come round in time.'

She looked up at Snow and gave him a look of sneering disdain. What the hell did this smart-suited copper know about how she felt or anything else about her? He'd eased himself out of a cosy warm bed in a nice house to come down here and gawp at her: the druggie tart.

Snow read all the implications in the gesture, but he persevered. 'Look, I really need your help. It's important that I build up a picture of the events that occurred this evening. Will you help me?'

'Do I have a choice?'

'In the end, not really. You could be awkward, I suppose, but that's likely to do you more harm than good. We just want to know what happened. You're not in any trouble here, but you are a very

important person – a witness to a violent crime. You could help us catch the person who did it.'

Gwen looked up and was surprised at the softness of his tone and the copper's kind expression. 'Go on, then,' she said at length. 'Try me. What do you want to know?'

'How well did you know Simon Barraclough?'

She laughed. It was guttural mirthless laugh filled with irony and bitterness. 'I didn't know him at all. He was a client. A punter. He paid me to be with him. That's the only fucking reason I was with the slime ball. I needed some cash.'

'He picked you up?'

'Yes, that's right. In the Shoehorn.'

Snow nodded. He knew it, a cellar bar on the main street in town. It was well known as a place where you could easily pick up a prostitute or buy certain substances.

'You'd not met him before?'

Gwen shook her head. 'No. If I had I'd not have gone with him. He was a bloody ignorant animal. Most of the blokes I go with at least attempt some kind of decent behaviour, but he treated me like dirt'.

'What happened when you got back to his bedsit?'

'Well, what do you think happened? We played snakes and ladders?'

'You know what I mean.'

Gwen shrugged. 'Yeah, well… We did the business and just as we were getting dressed there was this racket at the door. Someone was hammering away. This Simon goes to answer it and then everything went quiet for a bit and then I hears a kind of cry and a weird sound as though someone is gargling. Crazy. I was really scared by now and I just peered round the corner of the room down the passage and see… well, I see Simon on the floor and this bloke standing over him with a knife.'

'What did he look like – 'this bloke'?'

'I dunno. The light was behind him. He was all in shadow. He was like a shadow himself, a moving shadow.' She giggled erratically.

Snow waited for her to calm down before he spoke further. 'Come on, think, Gwen. There must be something you can tell me about his appearance. Was he tall or short, fat or thin?'

The girl pursed her lips and thought for a moment. 'Well, he looked tall and on the thin side. I'd say his hair was greyish. The light created a kind of halo and it looked fluffy and grey.'

'What about his face?'

'Nah. I couldn't see nothin'. As I said, it was all in shadow. Just a blank, black face.'

'Did you hear his voice?'

'No. I don't think he spoke.'

'What about his clothes?'

'Some sort of long mac or overcoat. Yeah, overcoat. I remember his shoulders. They were tweedy-like.'

Snow nodded. 'You're doing well. Now do think hard. Is there anything else you can tell me about his appearance? Anything at all.'

Gwen pretended to think and then shook her head. 'No, that's it. I was too scared to stay looking. I just glimpsed what was happening and got out of the way. I didn't want him to see me. I reckon he didn't know I was there or else I wouldn't be talking to you now.' She paused a moment, her brow softly folding into a frown. 'There was one thing though. It was kind of strange.'

'What was that?'

'Well, he'd killed Simon and that. Stabbed him to death hadn't he?'

'Yes.'

'Well, he seemed to be calm about it. He didn't seem angry or agitated. Not violent, like. He just did it and left.'

Some thirty minutes later, Snow was sipping a strong black coffee at his desk in his office reading the file on Simon Barraclough when Bob Fellows came in. 'I've taken a statement from the girl. Sparky little thing, she is. Is it OK if we let her go for the time being?' he said wearily.

Snow nodded. 'Yes. She's told us all she knows, which is precious little.' He gave a heavy sigh. 'Make sure we have full details of where she's staying. We need to keep her on our radar.'

'Right you are.'

'I don't think she's in any danger,' continued Snow. 'It's fairly clear our man didn't see her, but we must keep her name out of the papers just in case.'

'Sure.' Fellows perched on the edge of the desk. 'It doesn't get any clearer, does it?'

'No it doesn't.' Snow ran his fingers through his hair and sighed. 'There's no thread which links these murders. Well, no visible thread at least. But there must be one. There must. I'm convinced there is a purpose behind the killings. They are not random. The victims are connected in some way and have been picked out for a reason.'

'But what reason?'

'When we know that…' Snow left the sentence dangling and took a long slug of hot coffee.

Fellows glanced at his watch. 'Blimey, it's nearly three o'clock. It's hardly worth going home.'

'Nah, Bob, release the girl and then you get off. I reckon you've earned a bit of a lie in. We don't want that cold rearing its snotty head again, do we?'

Fellows needed no further prompting. He hopped off the desk and headed for the door. 'Never look a gift horse...' were his parting words.

Snow got up and walked to the window and gazed down at the empty street but his mind was focused on the case and in particular the unfathomable link that connected the three victims. It appeared that they didn't know each other, they came from different backgrounds and locations. And yet... And yet they must have something in common – however tenuous, however fragile. Something that gave a motive for murder. As he pondered this conundrum, one of the street lights below flickered erratically and then suddenly went out. As he stared at the defunct lamp something clicked in his brain. The bright light had faded, shrouding that particular patch of road in darkness, and this had given him the germ of an idea. It was crazy, off the wall, metaphorical – but it was something to cling on to. He rushed to his desk and began to scribble down a list of facts. The faster he wrote, the broader his smile grew.

CHAPTER EIGHTEEN

Despite the hectic and demanding nature of her job, especially at this time of year with Christmas fast approaching, Matilda was relieved when she drove through the school gates and manoeuvred her car through the throng of pupils to her reserved parking space. Whatever the day threw at her she knew she had the stamina, knowledge and wherewithal to be able to cope. This was her domain and she felt safe and secure here. Not like at home. It was no longer the haven it had once been. It was no longer her space. Roger was there.

After their confrontation the other evening there had been a kind of awkward truce between the two of them. Since then her brother had behaved well, been quiet, reasonably tidy and deferential; but somehow this unnatural behaviour was strangely intimidating. It created its own suspenseful atmosphere, making Matilda all the more nervous and apprehensive. It was like waiting for a bomb to go off. And she knew, knew of old, that something would go dramatically awry before long. She hated being in the house, in her own home, and she hated being around Roger. She prayed that he would stick to his word and be gone within a fortnight. Then she would try and claim her old life back.

It's funny, she mused bitterly as she brought her car to a gentle halt, you never appreciate normality until it is taken away from you. There was something safe and comforting about the mundane. She made her way to her office in her usual brisk fashion, nodding and smiling to her students and the odd member of staff she encountered en route.

Once inside her office, she rang through to her secretary. 'Good morning Maisie. I'd love a cup of tea. Is that possible?'

Maisie who was 'a treasure' replied in the affirmative.

Minutes later Maisie entered with the tea on a tray. 'Earl Grey with a chocolate digestive,' she said, smiling gently.

'That's wonderful,' said Matilda. 'I left home in a bit of a hurry this morning and didn't get chance for a cuppa there.'

Maisie nodded and was about to leave when she hesitated by the door. 'Sorry to be a bother but I've been meaning to ask you if you'd like to buy some raffle tickets. It's for St Peter's Children's Hospice.'

Matilda smiled gently. 'Of course.' She knew that the hospice was very close to Maisie's heart – her niece had had been there.

'They're sixty pence each or ten for a fiver.'

'I'll take ten.' Matilda reached for her bag and dipped inside for her purse. On opening it she discovered it was virtually empty. There just a few coins, her credit card and the card of a taxi firm she sometimes used. For a moment she did not know what to say as her brain tried to work out the mystery. 'It seems I forgot to bring some money with me,' she said at length, with a half-smile, realising how lame it sounded. 'Honest,' she added laughing, trying to make a joke out of it. 'I'll buy some tomorrow. I promise.'

'That's fine,' said Maisie easily. She knew Matilda well enough to believe her.

Once she was alone, Matilda sat back in her chair, her heart pounding. Despair and anger fought within her for mastery. There really was only one explanation why there was no money in her purse. Someone had taken it. There must have been at least forty pounds in there in notes. And there was only one person who could be responsible.

She clenched her fists in frustrated fury. Her own brother had stolen from her. She gave an exasperated cry. The bastard. He was beyond the pale. He'd had the gall to do this when he knew that he would be found out. His arrogance knew no bounds. She shook her head in disbelief. What the hell should she do about him?

On impulse, she picked up her phone and dialled. She got through to police headquarters quickly and asked to speak to Detective Inspector Snow on an urgent matter. Well, she thought, justifying the phrase, it was urgent to her. After a short wait, she heard Paul's voice at the other end.

'Paul, it's me, Matilda.'

'Matilda.' He sounded surprised. There was an awkward pause and then he said, 'Are you all right?'

'Yes, yes. Well no.'

'What on earth is it? What's the matter?'

She was beginning to regret being so impulsive and making the call. 'I can't talk about it on the telephone. Could we meet up?'

'Of course. When?'

'I can't get away until the end of school today. Could we perhaps meet for a drink in the bar of the George Hotel around five this evening?'

'Are you sure you're all right? You sound… somewhat upset. I could come to the school if you want.' She was touched by the concern in his voice.

'No, no. It's not that urgent. It's… It's just something… Something I want your advice about. This evening will be fine.'

'O.K. The George at five.'

'Thank you, Paul.' She paused and then added, 'It'll be good to see you again.'

After replacing the receiver, she opened her purse again and gazed at it, her anger firing up once more. 'The bastard.' She said the word out loud this time as she snapped the purse shut with a sudden violent motion.

Paul had mixed emotions as he approached the George Hotel just before five o'clock that evening. He was very tired, not having been home to bed since visiting the crime scene at the bedsit in New North Road. He'd grabbed a few hours' sleep in his chair but that was hardly refreshing, so now he felt fully knackered and he had a raging headache. He had thought he might nip home, shower and put on fresh clothes for this meeting (was it a date?) but he just hadn't had the time. He had shaved in cold water with a little plastic razor he kept in his desk for such occasions but he was fully aware that he looked rough, with a rumpled suit and a wrinkled shirt.

As he entered the foyer of the hotel and passed by the over-decorated Christmas tree laden with its cheap plastic trinkets and gaudy lights and made his way to the bar, he wondered again what Matilda wanted to see him about. Was she in some sort of trouble or was she about to end their relationship? Had she been building up to this emotional meeting of severance? Well, he reasoned, he would soon find out.

The bar was gloomy and empty except for one figure sitting alone at the far end. It was Matilda. She rose as he entered and gave him a wan smile. They embraced in a perfunctory manner.

'Thanks for coming,' she said, taking in Snow's less than smooth appearance. She had never seen him look so tired and dishevelled.

Snow glanced back at the bar. There was no one behind the counter.

'You have to ring for the barman,' Matilda said. 'It's hardly rush hour in here.'

'What can I get you?'

'A G and T if possible.'

It took a while for a callow youth to appear behind the bar and serve him. He performed his duties at a snail's pace without enthusiasm or charm. No wonder there are no customers, thought Paul.

'Thanks for coming,' Matilda repeated, as Snow handed her the gin and tonic.

'So,' he said, 'what's this all about?'

She sighed and shook her head. All day she had tried to work out what to say to Paul and, indeed, what she hoped would result from this meeting. Just before leaving school, she had begun to panic. Really she shouldn't involve him. Despite their relationship, he was a policeman after all. She didn't want to get Roger in trouble with the authorities. That would only exacerbate her problems.

Snow could see that she was in some form of distress but his professional experience told not to prompt or interfere. He waited.

'I have a brother: Roger,' she began and then paused, struggling compose the next part of her story. 'He's three years younger than me,' she added before pausing again.

Snow leaned forward and took her hand and gave it a gentle squeeze of encouragement.

'We were close as children but drew apart in our teens. I lost close contact with him when I was at university. By this time both my parents were dead. Roger's a headstrong, wayward character and got into all kind of scrapes. And then he got into drugs and dealing. He ended up in prison. It was while he was serving time, that he decided that he wanted to cut off all connections with his old life – with me I suppose. He wrote to me saying that he didn't want to see me again. To some extent this was a relief. We had grown so much apart that there was no real connection between us any more. I concurred with his wishes and got on with my life. As time went on I had almost forgotten about him. I suppose I blanked him out of my well-ordered respectable life. And then just over a week ago, he turned up on my doorstep expecting me to take him in while he sorted himself out. It was as though his rejection of me had never happened. What could I do? Despite everything he is my brother. He swears he has gone straight and is off the drugs but he's irresponsible and somehow I feel threatened by his presence.'

So that was the voice I'd heard on the telephone, thought Snow. Her brother. 'Has he harmed you?'

'Oh, no, nothing like that. He's said he will find a place of his own and get a job but he shows no sign of doing either and then today I found that he's stolen money from my purse. It was a crazy thing to do. He must know that he'd be found out. It was an abusive, brazen act.' Her eyes moistened. 'I just don't know what to do. I feel guilty about my feelings towards him – I cannot forget that he is my brother, but at the same time I just want him out of my life.'

She had started to cry now and withdrawing her hand from Snow's she scrabbled in her bag for a handkerchief. She dabbed her eyes and blew her nose before continuing. 'I don't know why I'm telling you this really. But I just needed to talk to someone and… maybe get their advice.'

'How much money did he take?'

'Only about forty pounds. It's not really the amount of money but the act. The invasion of my privacy. He seems to have taken over my house and my life. What should I do?'

Snow did not know what she should do, but he was not about to admit this. He thought for a second, covering his uncertainty by taking a drink. 'Shall I have a word with him?' He held up his hand before Matilda could respond. 'Not in my capacity as a policeman but as your friend. Does he know about me?'

Matilda shook her head. 'I've told him nothing about my private life.'

'Is that why you've not seen me?'

'Yes,' she said, lowering her eyes. 'It's stupid, I know but he's invaded enough of my personal space, I wanted to keep as much separate from him as possible.'

'Maybe if he knows there's a male friend in your life (Snow shied away from the term 'boyfriend') he will back off and do as he says and find his own place and friends.'

'Oh, he has no problem in finding friends. He brought one back to the house only a few days after arriving. I use the word friends loosely.'

'A woman he'd picked up?'

'No a man. Roger is gay.'

A shiver ran down Snow's spine. 'Oh,' he said.

'His sexuality has always fuelled his wayward ways. He knows he's different so he wants to build on it.'

Snow wanted to say that it did not have to be like that. Being gay does not necessarily make you a rebel. But he didn't. He knew that each individual coped with this predilection in his own way. Staying in the closet – hiding in the closet as he did - would be seen by many gays as cowardly and hypocritical.

'A man with issues,' Snow observed quietly. 'So, would you like me to have a word with him? As I say, not as a policeman but as your friend.'

'I'm not sure. Would it do any good?'

Snow shrugged. 'I can't say. It's difficult as I don't know the man but I should think it can't do any harm at least. It will show him that you are not alone or as vulnerable as it would seem he thinks you are. Snatching money from your purse could be just the beginning. This needs nipping in the bud.'

'You're right,' she said nodding in affirmation, her eyes brightening. 'Would you come back to the house with me now? Just to support me when I challenge him about the theft?'

'Of course.'

She leaned forward and kissed him gently on the cheek. 'Thank you.'

They drove out to Matilda's house in their separate cars. Snow was grateful for the time alone to allow him to sift through the information he had just been given. He felt very uncomfortable about the whole situation. It was not just because Roger was gay, although that increased his edginess, but he disliked the idea of becoming involved in this tangled domestic situation. He was used to dealing with such scenarios in his professional life where he was able to take an authoritative and objective stance but this was different. Very different. He had no idea what he could say to this man. He had a farcical vision of himself acting like a tough guy in a B movie western threatening the fellow, telling to leave town on the next stage and never darken Matilda's doorstep again. Despite himself, he smiled at the idea. Well, he thought, forcing himself to consider the situation philosophically, he would have to play it by ear, as they say.

He parked on the road outside Matilda's house rather than go up the drive and joined her on the porch. All the lights in the downstairs rooms were lit.

'He's home,' she said, her features taut.

They entered the hallway. The house was warm and welcoming. There was music playing in one of the rooms. Snow could also smell food, the pleasant aroma of home cooking.

A man emerged from the sitting room and greeted them. He was tall, with sharp angular features and long wavy blonde hair. It was clear from the large eyes and generous lips that this was indeed Matilda's brother. He smiled broadly, completely unfazed by Snow's presence.

'Oh, Mat, you're late. Another ten minutes and the food would have been ruined. And you've brought a guest. How naughty of you not to tell me. Still there will be enough to go round I reckon.'

Matilda opened her mouth to speak but no words came. Snow could see that she was non-plussed by this strange turn of events.

'Aren't you going to introduce me, Mat?' Roger said moving forward and holding out his hand to Snow. 'I'm Roger, Mat's brother, the black sheep of the family, but you probably know that.' He gave Snow a charming smile as the two men shook hands.

Matilda broke her trance and said, 'This is Paul. A friend.'

'Pleased to meet you, Paul, a friend. You will stay for dinner I hope. I've cooked a little something as a thank you and…' He took Matilda in his arms and gave her a kiss. '…an apology. I shouldn't have taken that money. It was a naughty and foolish thing to do.' He fished inside his jacket pocket and pulled out a wad of notes. 'Here you are, darling, the returned loot with interest. I had a bit of luck on the gee gees.'

He pressed the money into Matilda's hand before she could respond. 'Now you two go and take a seat in the lounge and I'll get you both a drink. Then I must away into kitchen or my gourmet delight may end up in the bin.'

After Snow and Matilda had been left alone, Matilda gave a mirthless chuckle. 'It's all an act of course.'

Snow could see that but it was a very smooth and accomplished one. Roger's apology and charm offensive had taken Matilda completely by surprise and had effectively pulled the rug from under her. Her brother now had no case to answer.

'Well,' said Snow slowly, 'it does make my role somewhat redundant now. I can't go wagging a finger after that little performance.' He tested a gentle smile out on her. 'Can I?'

She responded in kind, her eyes twinkling. 'I guess not, but trust me this is only a respite.'

'You know you can always call on me for help if needed.'

'Thank you, Paul.' She drew close and kissed him full on the lips.

'And now, I think I really ought to go.'

'Not on your life. You will stay and eat. I'm determined to make Roger keep up his charade all evening, which he'll have to do if you are here. And besides it will be awfully rude of you to leave after being invited to stay.' She tweaked his chin playfully.

Surprisingly Snow found the food very pleasant. It was a simple pasta dish but fresh and appetising. It was one of the best meals he had tasted in a while. At least it hadn't come out of a tin or from a packet which was *de rigueur* in the Snow household. For Matilda the whole occasion had a strange surreal air about it as though she was taking part in a Harold Pinter play: three people seated around a dinner table indulging in strained almost monosyllabic conversation that was masking true emotions and intentions. She was still angry with Roger. No amount of smarm and charm would excuse him for taking money from her purse. What would have been the scenario if the bloody 'gee gees' hadn't come in? Would he have shifted into the 'begging for forgiveness' mode? She also felt sorry for Paul. It wasn't really fair involving him in her

private family problems. He seemed to be coping on the surface, but she wondered how comfortable he felt beneath his apparently calm exterior.

Snow placed his knife and fork neatly on his empty plate and took a sip of water. 'That was excellent,' he said. 'Where did you learn your culinary skills?' he asked Roger.

'In the nick. Cookery classes *a la* Wandsworth. It's amazing what you can learn when you're banged up. Oh, I'm sure Mat has told you that I've been a very naughty boy, a lot worse than borrowing some money from her purse. But I'm a reformed character. Honest. And I enjoy cooking. I like the creative part. You take a set of disparate ingredients, put them together and come up with something that fills a plate with colour and a fine aroma, something that you can share with others.' He grinned broadly and reached out with his hand to touch that of his sister who had been very quiet during the meal. Giving him a frosty stare, gently she removed her hand from his touch.

Roger was unfazed by Matilda's cool response and turned his gaze towards Snow, the eyes still twinkling lightly. 'And what do you do to earn an honest crust, Paul?'

'I'm a policeman.'

'Gosh. So had you come along to arrest me or beat me up or something?'

'I'd thought about it.'

Roger laughed. 'Well, I'll come quietly if that will help. But before then, who's for dessert? I've made a rather fabulous cheesecake, even if I do say so myself. You must try a slice.' With these words, he rose quickly from the table and disappeared into the kitchen.

Matilda rolled her eyes. While Snow understood her frustration, he could not help but be faintly amused by the situation. 'He's certainly a charmer,' he said softly.

'When he wants to be. When it's necessary.'

Snow nodded. 'Don't worry, I understand. Why not raise the question of his moving out while I'm here? I can be your witness to his responses.'

'His lies, you mean.'

'Maybe. Let's see how he copes.'

'Wriggles out of it, you mean.'

At this point Roger returned and with a flourish placed the dessert in the centre of the table. Paul thought that the cheesecake was 'rather fabulous' as described and the generous portions were eaten for the most part in silence. Matilda toyed with hers while she considered how to approach the topic of Roger's departure.

Eventually, she asked, 'How are your plans going for finding somewhere else to stay?'

'Great,' came the instant reply. 'I was going to tell you later but since you asked… I went to see a place today: a little flat.'

'And…'

'Well, it wasn't suitable. It was a bit poky and there were certain things that needed doing to it. DIY is not my territory. But the estate agent who showed me round said he'd got a more suitable property on his books and I'm going to see it tomorrow.'

'Where is it, this other flat?' asked Paul

There was a moment's hesitation before Roger replied. 'Do you know I can't remember. Not far from the centre of town.'

'Which estate agent?' Matilda's voice was even with just a trace of ice.

'Something and something. A pair of them. Nice offices on the high street.'

'Well,' said Paul affably, 'I hope this place you see tomorrow will be suitable. I am sure Matilda will be glad to have her old place back to herself.'

Roger's eyes narrowed and his features darkened for a moment and then the sun came out once more and beamed brightly. 'I understand. Never did relish the role of a gooseberry.'

Silence fell like a shroud upon the proceedings. Roger rose noisily, collecting up the dessert plates. 'Coffee, coffee, coffee. Be with you in a tick,' he cried before sweeping from the room.

'I suppose we should have expected that,' said Snow once they were alone again.

Matilda nodded. 'I suppose so. I'm sorry, Paul.'

'Nonsense. No harm done – in fact possibly the reverse. I suspect he's never been near a flat today, but now he knows the situation, that I'm on the scene...

'... and a policeman.'

'...yes, I'm sure he'll start searching.'

'I hope you are right.'

When Roger returned with the coffee, he also brought a brandy bottle with him. 'I hope I could persuade out guest to take a little snifter with me. I know Mat dislikes the stuff.'

Snow who had declined wine with the meal because he was driving was tempted by the brandy – it was a good label – and agreed.

'Well, if you'll excuse me,' said Matilda, 'I'll go and powder my nose.'

With Matilda out of the room, Roger's whole body relaxed, his shoulders drooped and he slumped lazily back in his chair. He had consumed a large quantity of wine with the meal but had maintained an appearance of sobriety until this moment. Paul reckoned he had already been at the brandy in the kitchen, especially after the mini-interrogation regarding the flats. Roger took a sip of brandy, his head moving gently from side to side and he sighed loudly. 'Great stuff. You miss this in the nick.'

Snow nodded.

'So, how long have you known Mat?'

'A few months, maybe four.'

'Lovely girl.'

'Yes.'

'You serious about her?'

Snow laughed out loud. 'Next you'll be asking me about my career prospects and enquiring if my intentions are honourable.'

Roger saw the joke and chuckled. 'Sorry. I didn't mean to... I am sure you are a nice man, Paul.'

'I try to be.'

Roger's hand moved across the table and touched Snow's. 'I'm sure you are. A lovely man.'

Snow felt an uncomfortable tingle as Roger's warm palm pressed down on his. He did not remove his hand. The two men gazed at each other in the fierce silence. Snow felt his mouth go dry as a strange but familiar sensation swept through his body.

Later, as he drove home, Paul Snow tried to blank from his memory all the events of that evening.

CHAPTER NINETEEN

Snow was at his desk early the next morning sifting through the various witness statements in a desperate and, he tried not to admit to himself, a rather futile attempt to discern if he'd missed anything, any small crumb that could give him a clue, help provide him with a lead in this totally baffling murder case.

The door of his office opened and Chief Superintendent Clayborough slipped in noiselessly.

'Morning, Paul.' The greeting was casual enough but the posture was stiff and intimidating, as Paul knew it was meant to be. He knew his boss of old.

'Sir,' said Snow, annoyed with himself for not being able to keep the note of apprehension out of his voice.

'Just wanted a word.'

Snow could guess what that word was.

'This case of yours. Any progress?'

Snow gave a slight grimace and shook his head. There was no point bullshitting this old hand. 'Not really, sir. Still in the dark, I'm afraid. There doesn't seem to be a pattern or any motive. There's no connections between the victims except…'

'Clayborough raised an eyebrow. 'Except…'

'They've all done bad things.'

'Bad things.' Clayborough sneered at vagueness of this phrase.

'What the hell do you mean by that?'

'Well, Tindall, the first victim, was guilty of beating his wife. The second, Sullivan, was having sex with his daughter. She was pregnant by him.'

'I see.' Clayborough seemed unimpressed. 'And the third?'

'Simon Barraclough was a ne'er do well. He'd served a term in gaol and was … just a wastrel.'

'Is that it? That's your linkage.'

Snow hesitated a moment before nodding. It was the first time he had actually verbalised this idea and he knew how lame it sounded. From the expression on Clayborough's face it was clear that he thought so, too.

'Using that theory, your killer could take his pick of half of Yorkshire'. He sighed heavily before continuing. 'Look, Paul, we have three bloody murders on our hands and no fucking progress is being made. You know what the press are saying: incompetent police bastards etc. The killer is laughing up his sleeve at us and we're expecting another body to be dumped on our doorstep any minute now. And all you've got for me is the idea that the victims have done 'bad things'. Christ almighty! It's time you pulled your bloody finger out, lad. We've got to nail this son of a bitch and soon. Is that understood?'

'Of course, sir,' came the terse reply. Snow could have said more, much more but it would have been pointless and regarded as insubordination. He understood Clayborough's frustration. God, he felt it himself in spades but you cannot make something out of nothing. And as far as he could see things at the moment, he had nothing.

'I expect progress… soon.' Clayborough gave his parting shot before disappearing as swiftly and as silently as he had arrived.

Snow closed his eyes, pursed his lips and swore.

The day wore on wearily. In the afternoon, Snow paid another visit to Mrs Tindall to see if he could extract any more information from her, pick up any ideas or notions why anyone would want to kill her husband. He thought of it as a futile excursion and it was. It was interesting, however, to observe the change in the woman and the house. She was dressed in bright clothes, probably new, with her hair tidy and shining. She even wore a little make up. The sitting room had been rearranged and was clean and tidy with a picture of Jesus hanging over the mantelpiece. She saw Snow take note of this and smiled.

'I've started going back to church again,' she said, smiling. 'I was brought up a Catholic, as was Samuel, but he lapsed, didn't like going to the church and didn't like me going either.' Her grin broadened. 'But now I'm back in the fold and it's helped to make a new woman of me. I am so much happier. Father Vincent has been so very kind to me. I feel part of a family again.'

Snow said that he was pleased for her, noting silently that the death of her husband was not only a welcome release for her but a kind of rebirth. For her his murder had been a good thing.

He took this thought back to town and to the County where he sat in the snug hunched over a solitary pint. He felt very low. It seemed to him that life was not only kicking him in the shins but in other parts of his anatomy as well. Perhaps it was time for him to hand over his badge like a worn out Sherriff in a B movie and ride out of town. He allowed himself a brief bleak smile at the concept.

'I thought I'd find you in here.'

It was Bob Fellows. He carried a pint in his hand and sat beside Snow. 'Any news? Any good news?'

'Nope. No news, good or bad. We have flat-lined in this case. It seems we are in the hands of the killer, just waiting for him to strike again.'

Bob took a large gulp of beer and wiped the froth from his lips. 'That will never do,' he said with mock cheerfulness. 'Cheer up, sir. We'll get a break soon.'

'And pigs might fly.'

'With modern technology, who knows? Anyway, I almost forgot why I am here. Someone left a message for you at the desk this afternoon.'

'Who was that?'

'Don't know. A bloke. He left this.' Bob held up an eggshell blue envelope with Snow's name on it and the words 'PERSONAL & PRIVATE' printed in the top left hand corner. 'Who knows, this could be our break.'

Snow took the envelope without comment, broke the seal and extracted a single sheet of matching notepaper which contained a handwritten message. He read it and then slipped it back in the envelope and put that in his inside pocket. 'Nothing to do with the case, Bob. As it said: personal and private.'

Bob looked surprised at the curt response and took another gulp of beer to cover his dismay at Snow's brusqueness. Don't shoot the messenger, mate, he thought.

Without another word, Snow rose and pushed his glass of beer towards Bob. 'You can finish that if you want. I have to go.'

Before Bob could respond, Snow had gone.

'Blimey, what's got into him,' Bob muttered to himself and then pulled Snow's half full glass nearer to his. 'Still, waste not want not.'

When Snow got to his car in the parking lot at HQ, he sat inside and read the note again. The handwriting was bold, elegant and delivered with a flourish: 'Hi Paul, please meet me in the bar of the George Hotel this evening at six. I gather it's one of your regular watering holes. It is most important. Please don't let me down.

Many thanks, Roger.'

Snow stared at the note for some time, the words blurring after a time while his mind considered the various implications of the message. Initially he wondered whether he should go, but he knew that he had to. Apart from anything else, his policeman's curiosity was aroused. Had the fool done something outrageous and was about to confess to him? If he had harmed or caused distress to Matilda… He found his body tensing at the thought.

No, he had to go. He glanced at his watch. It was just after five. He'd drive along town, park in the square and wait until the appointed time.

Just after six o'clock he entered the George Hotel. As he made his way through the foyer to the bar, he was well aware of the strange ironical coincidence that he had been here the previous night around the same time to meet Matilda and now here he was to rendezvous with her brother. The bar was just as sepulchral and empty as it had been the previous evening, empty that is except for a sleek-suited individual sitting by the door. It was Roger.

He rose as Snow entered. 'So glad you could make it,' he said in cheery greeting, his voice heavy with drink. 'I didn't know if you'd be arresting a drugs baron or something. Let me get you a drink.'

'I'm OK,' replied Snow flatly.

'Oh, come on, I've dragged you here, the least I can do is buy you a drink. Wine, beer?'

Snow shook his head. 'I'm fine. Now, what is this all about?'

'Well, at least sit down so I can tell you.'

Reluctantly Snow did as he was asked.

'That's better. First of all, I just wanted to put things straight between us. I really got the impression last night that you don't approve of me.' He flapped his hands in the air. 'Of course, I can understand that. I know I'm the bad penny turning up unexpectedly, inconveniently – but I don't mean to be.' He leaned forward and placed his hand on Snow's shoulder. 'Honest.'

'It would be good if you came to the point.'

'Sure.' Roger leaned back and took a sip of wine. 'You'll be pleased to know I've got me a place. A little bijou flatette. Rented, of course. Can't afford to think of buying at the moment.' He grinned broadly. 'You knew I was telling porkies last night about estate agents didn't you?'

'Yes.'

Roger laughed. 'Well, you are a detective after all.'

Despite himself, Snow smiled. There was something strangely charismatic and endearing about this man. Oh, he was in no doubt that Roger was a complete shit, what the Americans called a shyster, and that he was not to be trusted an inch, but he had a winning warmth and charming manner that coated the sham and the slick, paper thin pretentions with a kind of glamour that was both disarming and attractive.

'So, I have my own little den. Furnished and ready for occupancy. I intend to move in tomorrow and Matilda will be free of me.'

Not exactly, thought Snow. He might no longer be sharing a house with her but he was not far away, lurking in the shadows of her life. Still, if he was telling the truth and had in fact rented a place of his own, that was a good thing, a move in the right direction, and it certainly would be a great relief for Matilda.

'Whereabouts is this flat?' asked Snow, realising that he was sounding like a policeman interrogating a suspect.

'It's a newish block at Chesil Bank, up Lindley way. I'd like to show it to you. See if you think I've done the right thing.'

'Show it to me?'

'Yes. Before Matilda sees it. That is if she'll visit me. I'm not used to taking on these kind of commitments recently. A few years in

jug makes you more than a bit rusty coping with normal, everyday things like… well, like renting a flat. I'd like to know if you think I've done the right thing. Get your opinion.'

Snow's expression suggested that he was baffled by this request. He was baffled but suspicious, too. Nevertheless, he reasoned, it would be good to affirm that Roger had indeed taken on a flat and was ready to move out.

Roger withdrew a set of keys from his pocket and dangled them before Snow.

'Number three, Chesil Court. Come and have a gander, Paul.'

Snow looked at his watch. 'Very well, but let's make it quick.'

Roger quickly drained his glass. 'Good man. Taxi or your car, I'm afraid. No wheels at present.'

'My car.'

Chesil Court was a three story rabbit hutch which had been built in the late sixties. It was a featureless utilitarian structure. There was an odour in the air, a mixture of damp, sweat and something else that assailed the nostrils as they entered the chilly foyer. Snow reasoned that only a desperate soul would want to live here.

Roger was still giving his upbeat performance. 'I'm afraid the lift is out of order at the moment, but I'm only on the second floor.' He took Snow's arm and guided him to the stone steps. The air was even more pungent here.

They came to a flat brown door with the number three in gold letters on it.

So it did exist, thought Snow. The man really was making an effort.

It was a poky little place with a small kitchen, a sitting room, bathroom and bedroom. The previous tenant had a penchant for flowered wallpaper, which dominated the sitting room and bedroom.

'Oh, I know,' said Roger with a flourish waving an arm extravagantly, 'that wallpaper. Ugh. As dear Oscar said, either that wallpaper goes or I do.' He laughed merrily. 'So what do you think of the old homestead. Kind of quaint, isn't it?'

Quaint was not the word that Snow had in mind.

'Well, I think you can guess what I think,' he said simply, 'but it will do as a stop gap measure, I'm sure, until you can get back on your feet again.'

'You're dead right. You are a clever cookie, Paul. Stop gap measure, indeed. Come on here and sit down here beside me.' Roger beckoned to Snow, and patted the bed.

'I'm OK.'

'Oh, I know you're OK. You're more than OK. In my eyes you are a pretty boy. A pretty, pretty boy. If you know what I mean.'

Snow said nothing but was unhappy about this sudden change in the conversation.

'You see, what I mean to say is not that you are not exactly pretty,' continued Roger. 'That would be silly. What I really mean is that I find you attractive. The cool exterior with that thin pale face, tense lips and those oh so hungry eyes. I don't know what they are hungry for... or perhaps I do. I have an inbuilt radar, you see. It comes as part of the equipment. Well, it does in my case. A gay radar and when I look at you, the needle is throbbing. Whizzing across the dial it is. The minute you walked into Mat's house last night, I sensed it. That louche way of walking, those gentle hand movements, that sensitive face which constantly radiates a vast array of changing emotions – as it is doing now.'

Snow shifted uneasily. 'I don't know what game you are playing, but I suggest you abandon it now.'

'Oh, Pauley, don't... don't be petulant. It's you who's playing the game. Remember what the bard said? 'To thine own self be true'...'

Roger rose from the bed and moved towards Snow, who instinctively took a step back. Roger beamed. 'I can't believe you are frightened of me. Really! Or is it yourself you are frightened of, eh? Frightened to let the true Pauley out of the closet.' With a sudden, swift movement, Roger grabbed Snow by the arms, pulling him forward and then he kissed him full on the lips.

With a snarl, Snow pushed Roger away and punched him hard on the chin. He fell backwards on to the bed, where he lay still for a few seconds before his body began to shake as though it was caught in some uncontrollable trembling fit. It took Snow some time to realise that in fact Roger was convulsed with silent laughter. At length he sat up on the bed, his eyes moist with merriment.

'Well, that wasn't the response I was expecting or hoping for.' He rubbed his chin and smiled. 'I suggest we finish the therapy session for today and continue it another time.'

Snow raised his fist again and Roger held up his arms in a protective gesture. 'Peace, brother. One punch is enough to cool my ardour, I can assure you.'

'You do that again and I'll arrest you for assault.'

'Mmm, well that might not go down too well at headquarters, eh? Might raise a few eyebrows. Confirm a few suspicions, eh?'

Snow really wanted to batter him now, but with great effort he pulled in his horns. When anger threatened to overwhelm his common sense, Snow had the great facility to step back from the situation and assess the fallout if he allowed his emotions their full rein. In this case, part of this mental assessment concerned a series of questions which disturbed him: why are you angry in the first place? Is it because you have been assaulted in a minor way? Is it because Roger has quite accurately assessed your sexual predilections? Is it because the kiss did not disgust you?

Snow was afraid of the answers.

He realised that the only sensible course of action for the moment was to escape from the situation. Escape. It seemed cowardly to him to think of it in those terms, but it was also prudent. Without another word, he turned on his heel and left the flat. Two images fought for prominence in his mind as he made his way down the rank smelling stairs to the fresh air beyond: his last view of Roger sitting on the bed, his hair rumpled and tie askew, a broad knowing grin on his face; and that kiss – the warm moist force of it on his lips.

That night Paul Snow lay awake unable to sleep. The incident with Roger in his flat had disturbed him greatly and part of his mind would not fully admit why. That way madness lies, he told himself. He kept running the scene over and over in his mind, reducing the images to slow motion when it came to that kiss. He felt it as though it were happening all over again and he felt his body stiffen with emotion. Oh, shit, his mind screamed as he sensed that his own personal walls of Jericho were starting to crumble.

CHAPTER TWENTY

Lucy Anderson walked down the street in what would seem to a casual observer as a nonchalant if rather robotic fashion. She was carrying a large canvas shopping bag which bore the legend 'Love Life. Eat Well.' Inside the bulging bag, well protected by several plastic bags and newspaper was the body of a dead baby.

She shouldn't have done it. She should have controlled herself. It was a moment of madness.

It was murder.

She gulped awkwardly at the thought of that word and fierce hot tears sprang to her eyes. She wiped them away quickly with her free hand. She mustn't draw attention to herself. No one must suspect her. No one must look at her. Wonder what was in the bag. It was groceries, dummy. Just groceries. What else? It's a bloody shopping bag.

The deed was done now and so she had to get rid of the evidence.

In her disturbed state Lucy Anderson did not see herself as a bad woman. She had been driven to do what she did. If only the baby had stopped crying. No one could put up with that. Crying, crying, crying... Its constant scream had pierced her brain until she hadn't been able to think straight. It was like a shrieking drill boring into her head. No matter what she did – hugs, rocking, feeding, toys – the crying did not stop. It was ceaseless. There was no respite. Her medication didn't help, even though she upped her dosage in an attempt to ease her pain. In the end she came to believe the baby was doing it deliberately. Punishing her. It was a demon child sent to torment her for her sins.

She peered over the cot, gazing at that shrieking shiny, red-faced brat with all the facial contortions of a gargoyle. Yes, there could be no doubt this thing was plaguing her on purpose. It was its mission to drive her mad. She made the sign of the cross over the child and this only seemed to increase the volume of its yells. She warned the foul thing that if it did not 'shut the fuck up, it will be the worse for you', but the creature took notice. It blithely ignored the warning and carried on crying.

She put the cot in the airing cupboard and shut the door on it, but she could still hear the child with its unrelenting banshee wails.

It was then that she snapped. It had to die. That was the solution. That would bring silence and calm back once more. With this realisation she felt a refreshing serenity possess her. With slow precision she took the child into her bedroom, still wriggling and bellowing. She saw it now not as a small human being but as an alien entity, a monster of evil, something disgusting that must be destroyed.

With slow precise movements, she took one of the pillows from her bed and, gently at first, placed it over the baby's face. Once in position, she pushed down with great force. She felt the creature wriggle beneath her, but to her delight the cries eventually lessened. Until they stopped altogether, along with any movement. The thing lay still and silent. She stayed with the pillow pressing down on the dead child for over a minute just to be sure. And then slowly she removed it and gazed down on the fragile form on the bed, its little mouth still open, eyes bulging, but silent now.

At first, she smiled, even chuckled at her success in stopping the noise, that piercing stiletto shriek jabbing in her ears was now replaced by a strange hissing silence. It was wonderful. And then, as night time shadows faded with the morning light, the reality of what she had done broke over her like a giant wave. Her body shook as she realised the full horror of her actions. Ice filled her veins and she choked on her own agonised cries. In desperation, she snatched up the baby and hugged it to her breast, showering its tiny head with kisses in the vain hope of reviving the child. But it remained a corpse, limp and lifeless in her tight embrace. She sank to the floor sobbing, still clasping the baby to her bosom.

She stayed like that for some considerable time. At length the tears subsided, but she remained, like a hunched statue, crouching by the bed with her tiny daughter. Gradually, sleep overcame her and she slipped into unconsciousness for an hour. When she awoke, she was cold, shivering and groggy. Then she saw the baby in her arms and the horror of her actions came back to her again.

The next day was like a living nightmare. She placed the baby in its crib and tried to act normally. She tried watching television but her mind kept slipping back to her corpse child. She constantly returned to the crib to gaze down at the baby, half hoping that she had been mistaken. She wasn't really dead, just asleep. It would wake soon and begin to cry again. But the face was immobile, twisted into that silent scream and now the face had begun to turn blue.

It was then that Lucy's sense of self-preservation and survival began to rise within her. She knew that she could not leave the thing in the flat. She had to get rid of the body – for that is what it was now: just a dead thing. She was brave enough now to think of it in those terms. It was dead. There was no going back on that. She hadn't meant to kill it but, God forgive her, she had and no doubt he would take out his own punishment on her. In the meantime, she had to dispose of the thing before it began to decompose and smell. She hated bad smells.

By the time she began to assemble the packing material, all emotion had drained from her mind and body. She moved methodically, precisely and stoically as though she was preparing a parcel for the post. She placed the baby inside a large plastic bag to begin with and taped that up securely. She then placed this inside another, thick plastic bag and continued this process until she had completely obliterated the shape of the little body inside. She then lowered this into the large canvas shopping bag and covered it up with old newspapers.

She stood back to admire her handiwork and smiled a crooked smile. No one would ever suspect that the bag held a dead baby.

Now she was walking down a street at the other side of town, far away from her own little flat. Soon she came to the building she wanted: the Wah Yung Chinese Restaurant. She'd had many of their cheap special lunches in there – so called 'business lunches' although she had no business. Slipping down the side street at the far right of the restaurant and checking that there was no one else in sight, she entered the yard at the back of the premises. It was here that there were two large industrial-sized garbage bins, receptacles for the restaurant's waste. She glanced round to ascertain that the place was deserted and then placing the shopping back on the ground, she heaved the large lid up on one of the bins exposing the rotting contents. A pungent aroma escaped, assailing her nostrils. She gagged momentarily and stepped back. The inconsequential thought crossed her mind that it was fortunate this wasn't summer for with the heat the stench would be more powerful and there would be a strong likelihood of flies and maggots to contend with.

Swiftly, she retrieved the shopping bag from the floor and emptied the wrapped contents into the bin. It slipped in easily, the weight causing it to sink down. Lucy leaned over the edge of the bin and pulled some of the stinking detritus over the top of the bundle to cover it up. This close contact with the rotting food made her gorge rise and it was with a gasp of relief that she was able to pull back and allow the lid to close again. She gazed at the bin for a moment. It was, she admitted, an unfitting grave for her baby, but a necessary one. God would forgive her, wouldn't he?

She left the yard and returned to the main street. She headed to the nearest public house. Alcohol would help to ease her guilt. Surely?

CHAPTER TWENTY ONE

Goodall's Garage (Servicing, Repairs & MOTs) was a small outfit housed under the arches of the viaducts on the appropriately named Viaduct Street at the far end of town. There were a number of vehicles parked outside the entrance – all of them at least three years old. Passing through the massive open sliding doors, Paul Snow found himself in a large, high-ceilinged gloomy chamber not unlike a small aircraft hangar. Fluorescent strip lights hung down from the ceiling providing some meagre illumination. At the far end was a hydraulic lift, holding an old Cortina. It was raised from the ground and two men in dark oil-stained overalls were working on the underside of it. One held a spot lamp while the other was adjusting something with a spanner.

A stout man in a red boilersuit came out of the box-like office built into the wall by the door and approached Snow. 'Can I help?' he said brusquely in an unsmiling manner that seemed to suggest to Snow that the man was intimating that he was trespassing on his premises.

Snow was happy to take the wind out of his sails. He held up his warrant card. 'Police,' he said in a tone that echoed that of the garage man.

The man in red overalls sighed as though to say, 'What now?'

'Mr Goodall?'

'Mr Goodall is dead. Been gone five years or so. I own the business now. Finch. Stewart Finch. Just kept the name on because the place had got a good reputation. What's the problem, officer?' There was almost a sneer on the word 'officer'.

'It's about Frank Sullivan.'

'Oh, him. Well, I had one of your boys round here asking about Frank only the other day. I told him all I knew.'

Which was nothing, thought Snow. He'd read the report, which noted that Sullivan was a decent worker if a bit slow. He kept himself to himself. Didn't give much away. Finch didn't even know which soccer team he supported. That was about it.

'Just thought I'd check things out again.'

Finch shrugged. He was obviously not impressed. 'Well, what d'you want? I've nothing more to give you.'

'You've no idea if Frank had any enemies – or friends even.'

Finch laughed derisively. 'This isn't a social club. It's a garage. We turn up at eight-thirty, fix a few cars and go home. End of story.'

'No one came to see him here. A man…. A woman?'

Finch grinned at the mention of a woman. 'A woman? Don't make me laugh.' He shook his head. 'I told the other copper, no one came here to see him.'

Snow could see that he was not going to get anywhere with this belligerent soul. Maybe he'd had an unpleasant experience with the police and he still bore the scars.

'Tell you what you can do,' Finch said suddenly as though a thought had just struck him. 'You can take his stuff away.'

'Stuff.'

'Aye, from his locker. There's some of his personal clobber in there. I don't want it and I reckoned if I chucked it out you'd be on my back. He's no close family to send it to, so you'd better have it.

I'll be needing the locker for the new bloke when I can find one. Good mechanics are like hen's teeth.'

'Let me have a look.'

Without a word, the garage man led Snow to a row of four rusting metal cabinets on the far wall and pulled open the door of the end one. It creaked noisily as he did so, filling the cavernous space with a high-pitched noise that sounded like a child's scream.

'That's his stuff,' said Finch.

His stuff did not amount to much. There was just a thermos flask and some heavy duty boots at the bottom of the cabinet. These were nestling on a small pile of girlie magazines. A pair of greasy dungarees hung from a hook inside and there was a picture of Jesus stuck to the back of the door. It was the same one that he'd seen in Sammy Tindall's house: a simple crude sentimentalised image in garish colours.

'I'll get a bag from my car and take these away,' said Snow.

'Good man,' replied Finch without enthusiasm.

As he bagged the contents of the cabinet up, Snow was convinced there was really nothing here that would aid him in his investigation. Well, except one thing. And once again he thought about that street light near his office suddenly going out and leaving the street in darkness.

CHAPTER TWENTY TWO

After the third vodka, she began to cry. She sat cradling the empty glass in the midday gloom of the Shoehorn Bar and allowed the silent tears to flow. She felt her mind ripple with a mixture of emotions, not quite sure why she was so upset. Was it relief, guilt, desperation at her shit life or just physical and emotional exhaustion that had brought on this lachrymose reaction? Whatever, the tears were a wonderful release – a kind of absolution. That was it. She considered this possibility for a few moments and then sniffed. Absolution? Was it buggery. Absolution, my arse. She was fantasising now. Surely it was self-pity that prompted the tears. She just felt bloody sorry for herself. Whatever, she knew two things: it was helping her adjust to what she had done and she needed another drink.

Wiping her face with her sleeve, she left her quiet, dim corner and made her way to the bar where the barman, an old bloke with long straggly white hair and a boozer's nose was smoking a roll up as he perused the sports pages of a tabloid newspaper.

She asked for another vodka. With a twitch of irritation at being disturbed from his analysis of the runners and riders and without giving Lucy a glance, he swiftly procured the drink and slapped it in the counter. 'One pound ten,' he said in the tones of a speak your weight machine.

She paid in small change, her meagre supply of cash now running very low, and retired to her shady corner to drink and contemplate her lot once more. The vodka helped but it began to put a different perspective on her outlook. Now guilt rose like a dark cloud on the horizon, enveloping her in its sable embrace. Remorse welled up inside her and once more she began to cry. 'Bloody hell,' she whispered to herself, between silent sobs, 'this can't go on. It just can't.'

The distance along New Street from the Shoehorn Bar to the far end of town and the police station is less than half a mile, but with three vodkas swilling inside her and the bitter December wind chilling her to the marrow, it seemed to Lucy like a marathon trek. Her feet shuffled on the pavement as the sharp frosty air mingled with the alcohol intensifying her inebriation. More than once she bumped into a passing pedestrian, uttering a muffled, belated slurry, 'Sorry', after they had moved on and were out of earshot.

When she reached the police station, she hesitated. Was she up to this? Could she really confess? Was that the answer she sought? She walked past the entrance and on to the end of the street before turning round and making her way back, her mind spinning with questions. Perhaps she needed another drink to give her that extra burst of courage. Either that or she shouldn't have had the last vodka.

As she vacillated on the pavement, a uniformed policewoman came up behind her. 'Can I help you, love?'

Lucy turned around startled. 'Help me?' she asked, not sure what the woman meant.

The policewoman narrowed her eyes. The voice and the alcoholic fumes told her that this girl was drunk.

'I've come to confess,' Lucy said with a sudden dramatic gesture.

'Have you now? It might be best to go home and sleep it off first.'

'No, no. I gotta do it now. Confess. You have got to let me confess.'

'OK, love,' said the police woman, taking Lucy's arm and gently guiding through the doors of the police station.

'Take a seat there and I'll get you a coffee.'

'I want to confess.'

'Of course you do. The officer at the counter, Constable Purvis over there, will take down your statement after you've had a coffee, eh?'

The policewoman turned to her colleague behind the desk, rolled her eyes and mouthed the word 'Pissed.'

Constable Purvis smiled and leaned over the counter. 'You sit a while, little lady. I'll attend to you shortly,' he said. Lucy did as she was told while the policewoman, who had escorted her in, disappeared through a door, presumably to get her a coffee. All of a sudden, Lucy began to feel clammy and uncomfortable. The room was stuffy and dimly lit by a single fluorescent tube and a small rectangular window high up on the outer wall. It had bars across it – like prison bars.

PC Purvis was attending to some paperwork on the counter as though he had already forgotten about this inebriated woman who wanted to confess. Slowly, with a kind of chilling awareness, Lucy began to realise the enormity of what she was about to do. And what would happen to her after she had unburdened herself. Suddenly, fear gripped her soul as a though her body had been placed in a huge vice. She shuddered so hard that she almost cried with the shock of it. Her eyes wandered up once more to the window and those bars. Dark streaks again the pale blue sky beyond.

Panic set in.

She had to escape. This had all been a terrible mistake. She had to get out – now! She rose quickly and made a move for the exit. The plastic chair scraped on the floor attracting the constable's attention. He saw the woman make for the door.

'Hey, miss,' he called out, but it was too late, she had gone.

As Lucy felt the cold air on her face again, she collided with a tall thin man in a blue overcoat who was carrying a black bin liner.

'Whoa,' he cried.

Lucy gazed up into his face. It was a kind face, she thought, if a little sad.

'Where are you going to in such a hurry?' he said.

For a moment her mind whirled and then she said, 'Bus. Mustn't miss my bus.' And pulling away from him quickly, she rushed off down the street.

Snow shrugged. His instinct was to go after her. Anyone leaving police HQ in such a hurry must raise one's suspicions but she seemed harmless enough and he didn't want to over-dramatise the situation. Just as Snow was about to enter the building, PC Purvis emerged, nearly bumping into him.

'Sorry, sir,' he said. 'I was trying to catch a young woman. Did you see her?'

'I did. She's hurried off down the street, possibly to the bus station.'

'Probably gone to sleep it off, more like.'

'What's it all about?'

Purvis shrugged. 'Piss artist. About to waste police time but changed her mind. We're used to them in the evenings, but not so much at lunch time.'

Snow nodded and made his way inside, casting the incident from his mind. He had other matters to concern him.

He took the bin liner up to his office, brewed himself a strong coffee and then dipping into the black plastic sack, pulled out the picture with the illustration of Jesus. It was a heavily sentimentalised portrait which, Snow felt sure, was meant to be used for domestic worship. A little do-it-yourself altar for the living room. Sure enough, there on the back was a rubber stamped logo: 'St Joseph's Church. Peace be with you.'

He stared at the picture long and hard. He knew what he had to do. It had to be worth a second try. Subtle, clever questioning, catching the fellow off guard might just reveal a little more information. With a bit of luck he might let slip more than he meant to. Snow shrugged. He had nothing to lose by trying. Confucius he say man without haystack grasps any straw. Snow smiled grimly to himself.

The afternoon was bright if bitterly cold with a flawless china blue sky which promised a hard frost that evening. Snow strolled casually through the churchyard, stopping every so often to read one of the ancient gravestones there. 'William Crowther, watchmaker of this parish, died 1874 and the age of forty two. A good man and true'. Forty two. Life was short then even for those who were allowed to run their natural course.

The church door was closed, but it opened quite easily when Snow turned the large rusty ring that hung down by the lock. The squeak of the hinges echoed inside like the call of some strange bird. The church, illuminated only by the shafts of daylight falling through the stained glass windows resembled a smoky etching, a scene which was both pleasing and somehow comforting to Snow. He was not a religious man but he had always enjoyed the serenity and hushed calming atmosphere of churches.

'Can I help?' A voice broke the silence.

Snow sought its owner. He found him standing on a tall step ladder by one of the light fittings at the right hand side of the door.

It was the brusque Brian Stead, the church warden, gazing down at him through his thick lenses.

'I said, can I help,' he repeated in a tone that suggested that the last thing he wanted to do was help.

'Hello, there Mr Stead…'

The church warden stiffened. It was clear he was surprised that this shadowy visitor knew his name.

'It's Inspector Snow. I was hoping to have a word with Father Vincent.'

'Oh, it's you.' With care, Arnold made his way down the step ladder. He came close to Snow peering at him as though to verify that he was indeed Inspector Snow and not an imposter. 'I think the Father is in the vestry attending to some business or other. If you'll come this way, I'll see if he has time to see you.'

Snow repressed a smile. 'That's very kind,' he said.

As they walked down the aisle towards the altar, Snow took the picture of Christ from his inside pocket. 'Tell me,' he said casually, 'are these pictures readily available to your parishioners?'

Stead twisted his head in the direction of the picture and with stiff mechanical actions, crossed himself. 'Not readily available. They cost money to print do them. Father Vincent has a stock of them and he gives them to some of those who come to confess. Well, I say he gives them. They're fifty pence. But, as you can see they're good quality. I've got one at home. It's good to be reminded that He's looking after you. That He's part of your life. Mind you some of the flotsam and jetsam that turn up for confession don't deserve His mercy or His forgiveness, I can tell you. They think if they spill the beans regarding the nastiness they've been doin' it's all right. Their slate will be wiped clean, ready for them to mess it up again.'

'And you think it hasn't been wiped clean?'

'Of course it hasn't. A bad deed is a bad deed. A few Hail Mary's won't wash the stain away. A wrong cannot be made right.'

'That's what your religion says.'

'Maybe. I am not so sure.'

'Is Father Vincent sure?'

Arnold opened his mouth and was about to say something when he shut it again. 'That's not for me to say. You'd best be asking him that. All I know is that worshipping Christ and being a good man is the moral way and those that stray don't deserve any kind of salvation. They're given a choice and if they take the wrong road it's their fault and they should pay.'

'That's rather harsh.'

'That's a strange point of view coming from a copper. You like to bang wrongs 'uns up don't you? You don't let 'em off lightly. There's no forgiveness there in a prison sentence. I see these folk coming to this church to see the Father, heads hanging down, mournful expression, tearful, the lot. Five minutes in that box and they skip out with a smile and a song. They use the confession as a kind of get out clause… Well that's my view anyway. You'd be surprised how many of 'em come back time after time to be let off the hook.' He gave an inarticulate growl and moved his hand in a swift dismissive action to indicate that was all he was going to say on the subject.

Snow took the hint. 'Are these pictures exclusive to this church?'

'I shouldn't think so. Father Francis gets them in. Again, you'd better ask him.'

By now they had reached the transept before the altar. 'Wait here,' said Stead, still maintaining his bluff tone as he disappeared through a side door.

Snow sat down on the front pew and inhaled, taking in that special air that one finds in old churches: it is cool, strangely scented, a mixture of incense, polish and a faint trace of damp. Snow found it uplifting. He gazed at the rich multi-coloured fragments in the stained glass windows, which glistened in the gloom. He was rather disappointed to have his reverie interrupted by the return of Brian Stead.

'Father Vincent says you can go through.'

Snow found the priest in the cramped vestry, hunched over an ancient gas ring. 'You've called at a very convenient time, Inspector. I am just about to make a pot of tea. Would you care to join me?'

Snow was not a great fan of tea but he knew it would be useful to the interview for him to be amenable. 'That would be most kind. Just a little milk and no sugar.'

Once the tea ceremony had been completed, both men were seated by the priest's desk which was laden with leaflets, piles of paper, various volumes and files. He saw Snow note the apparent paper chaos and smiled. 'I assure you there is a method in my filing system. I can lay my hands on anything I want without a search,' he said smiling.

'Do you have copies of these?' Snow produced the picture of Christ.

'Indeed, I have. Where did you get that one?'

'From the work locker of Frank Sullivan.'

'Ah, yes,' replied Father Vincent, his gentle features darkening. 'How did he come by it?'

'I gave it to him. As a comfort, when he came to see me.'

'When he came to confess.'

Father Vincent sighed. Snow was so persistent. 'To confessional. Yes,' he agreed, throwing the detective a crumb.

'To reveal all his sins.'

'It's what we do as Catholics. Do you have a faith yourself, Inspector?'

'No.'

'Ah, I see.'

'Why did Sullivan need comfort, the picture of Christ?'

'I would have thought that was obvious, Inspector. He had just lost his daughter in very distressing circumstances.'

'It had nothing to do with his sins?'

'I believe we have had this conversation before. You know very well that what Frank Sullivan said to me is…' The priest faltered and gave another sigh before taking a large gulp of tea. 'Look, Inspector,' he resumed, 'believe me I do not wish to hinder your investigations but you must understand and appreciate my position.' He paused again and Snow waited. 'Let me say this, I am sure that nothing Frank Sullivan said to me in confessional will have any bearing on the terrible murders that you are investigating. How could it? The man ended up dead himself.'

'But why? I'd like to know if he had any inkling that his life was in danger.'

'I don't believe he did. He was just a sinner seeking forgiveness. That's all I can say.'

'And did he receive forgiveness?'

'It's not for me to take on the role of our Lord. I listen and offer succour.'

'And provide a penance.'

'Yes, that is the route to forgiveness.'

'So no matter what foul sin a man may commit, he can be given a route to forgiveness, as you call it, an escape route.'

'If you want to put it like that, but it does not mean that he will receive full absolution from his sins.'

Snow left the priest uncertain whether the visit had been useful to him or not. Certainly on the surface he had learned little that was new but something the priest had said troubled him. He had always assumed that a confessional led to complete absolution. It seemed, however that Father Vincent thought differently.

As Snow made his way down the aisle on his way out of the church, Brian Stead emerged out of the shadows. 'I bet you got nowhere, eh, Inspector? Like a clam is Father Vincent. He won't reveal a word of what they say to him. I wish he would.'

'Why is that?' asked Snow casually.

'Well, they need to suffer, don't they? If they've committed a sin in the eyes of God, they need to pay for it with a bit of pain. Depending on what they've done.'

'What about murder? If they confess to murder?'

Stead grinned ghoulishly and drew his right forefinger across his throat.

CHAPTER TWENTY THREE

As Matilda drove home she was filled with a mixture of excitement and apprehension. She was going back to an empty house – she hoped. She had waved Roger off in a taxi that morning. He had taken with him the two suitcases containing all his worldly possessions. He was off to his new flat and giving her back her life. Initially, she had felt a tiny pang of guilt at pushing this filial cuckoo from her nest; but she very quickly recovered from that. She knew that her brother was still going to be there in the background and she feared that he would prove to be a problem from time to time, but at least now she had recovered the sanctuary of her own dwelling. And now perhaps she could resume her relationship with Paul and get that back on track.

As she turned her car up the drive, the thought struck her that maybe the whole thing was one of Roger's jokes. He had returned as soon as she had left the house and when she opened the door he would be standing there grinning at her, shouting, 'Surprise, surprise!' Although she knew this was nonsense she couldn't shake the unsettling idea from her mind as she approached her front door and unlocked it.

The house was empty. It was still, silent and thankfully Roger-free. There was, however, a bottle of champagne, a bunch of flowers and a note waiting for her in the kitchen. The sight of these chilled her. So he had returned. He had come back to the house after she had gone to work. She snatched up the note, scribbled in Roger's extravagant hand: 'Hey Sis, thanks for your kindness. You are no doubt delighted to have me out of your hair. Well, darling, you can relax now. And I promise you the new flat is just the first step on the complete rehabilitation of yours truly. But more importantly, I'd like you and Paul to come for dinner on Sat evening at my new pad. See you around 7.30. No excuses. Love R.'

Despite herself, Matilda smiled. This was followed by the return of the feelings of guilt. Perhaps she had misjudged her brother after all. Certainly, she now thought, she had been too hard on him. Could it be that he was about to do a reversal of the Jekyll and Hyde routine and actually convert into an honest and respectable citizen? Time would tell and she would have to be patient. Matilda slipped the champagne in the fridge and put the flowers in a vase in the hall and then poured herself a large white wine. Slipping her shoes off, she slumped into an armchair and sighed. Perhaps things were going to get better now. This thought collided with one about Paul. Could she really woo him back to her after this strange interlude? She had rather frozen him out of her life for a while. She now accepted that her frustrations and worries regarding Roger had turned her into an ice maiden where Paul was concerned. She had behaved badly and would need to practise some clever coaxing to get the relationship back on track. Certainly, she couldn't imagine an evening meal at Roger's place would hold any attractions for him.

On impulse, she slurped down the rest of the wine and rang Paul. She got the answer machine. She grimaced, but left a message.

After her abortive visit to the police station, Lucy had returned home and drank several cups of coffee. She felt awful both physically and mentally. Her mind was a mess. She was a mess. Her life was a mess. Well, she mused, what do you expect when you've just murdered your child? This brutal observation brought on another bout of crying. If only there was someone she could turn to. But there was no one. She had no family. There were a few casual friends but she could hardly reveal her dark secret to them. They would be appalled. They would inform the authorities.

She wandered about the tiny flat, running her hands through her hair, desperate for some comfort, some glimmer of light. Perhaps… perhaps she should pray…?

'I can recommend the chicken madras. It warms up a treat.'

Paul Snow turned his attention from the freezer cabinet in the Fine Fayre supermarket where he had been perusing the vast array of microwave meals for one to face the speaker. It was Roger. He was grinning broadly.

Snow found himself lost for words. He felt awkward and unprepared for this encounter. He really didn't know how to react to this man, not after their last meeting.

'Or perhaps that is a little too spicy for you,' Roger continued with a knowing wink.

'Perhaps,' Snow found himself saying.

'Miserable little things, aren't they? These meals for one. Made to be consumed by losers, billy-no-mates. For those who can't even find a companion to have a little nibble with. I've eaten my fair share so I should know. Surprised that you're after one though. Thought you might have been out on the town with Matilda celebrating.'

'Celebrating?'

'Getting me out of the way so that you could… carry on where you'd left off before I turned up and interrupted things.'

Snow turned back to the cabinet and picked up the chicken madras. 'This will do me tonight,' he said.

Roger laughed. 'A fellow of firm principles. I like that in a man.' He touched Snow's arm briefly. Snow took a small step back. 'Paul, will you do me a favour before you fly away to your manly chicken dish for one. Seriously…?'

Snow raised his brow in silent query.

'Come and have a drink with me now. Just a pint. As a kind of apology for my dreadful behaviour the other evening. I know I was crass and stupid. I really don't want there to be an awkward rift between us.'

Snow shook his head. 'I don't think…'

'Please, my dear chap. Just for me. I'm a 'meal for one' saddo too. I'm alone in this big old town. A bit of company for brief while. Just one pint, eh?' Roger touched Snow's arm again. This time he did not move.

It was early evening in the White Hart and the pub was abuzz with noise and clouded with cigarette smoke. It was filled with workers on their way home who had called in for the one drink and had stayed for more, along with old codgers who had been drinking slowly and quietly for most of the afternoon and the odd teenage group gearing up for a night out. Snow and Roger had walked there from the supermarket while Roger kept up a monologue of inconsequentialities and Snow remained silent. He wondered why the hell he had succumbed to the offer of a drink – a drink with this man of all people. Maybe it was because he was Matilda's brother – but that explanation did not really convince him. He was not normally that weak or indecisive. He was angry and disappointed with himself; but also - and this was more worrying - apprehensive. They found a seat in the far corner of the main bar after Roger had secured their drinks.

'Cheers,' grinned Roger, clinking Paul's glass. 'So glad I bumped into you. Rendezvous at the chiller cabinet, eh? And so glad you agreed to come for a drink.'

'Why?' asked Snow, gently.

'Ah, forever the policeman, eh? What was my motive, officer? Well, to clear the air, I suppose. As I said, I was a bit foolish the other night and I apologise but I do want us to be friends. I don't have many in this town. I don't have any, in fact. I've been away too long. It's not easy coming out of the nick and trying to start afresh you know.'

Snow nodded.

'I am serious about wanting to be a good boy, but you can't blame me for me being desirous of a little fun as well and to be honest I thought you might be up for it.'

'What on earth made you think that?' Snow had asked the question before he realised how dangerous it was.

'Your manner. Your whole… you. One knows… or at least I thought I did. It's a pity because I find you a rather lovely man and I'm into lovely men.' He laughed lightly and despite himself Snow smiled.

'I must admit I've never thought of myself in those terms.'

'Well, now you know. You should feel rather chuffed with yourself when both brother and sister fancy you.'

'I think it's time to change the subject. How are you settling in to your new place?'

'Well, it's hardly the Ritz but it will do for the time being. Still, you'll be able to see how I've tarted the place up a bit on Saturday. I've invited you and Mat for dinner.'

This was the first Snow had heard about it but he didn't say so.

'What's the situation on the job front?'

'I've got an interview on Friday with an insurance company -

just as a lowly desk jockey but, as I keep saying, it's a start.'

'I'm pleased for you.' And Snow surprised himself by actually meaning it.

At Roger's persuasion, the two men stayed on for a another drink and Snow's demeanour mellowed further. By the time they were draining their second pint, a casual observer might have assumed these were two old friends having a night out. Roger half rose from his chair lifting his empty glass. 'One for the road, eh?'

Snow shook his head. 'Better not. Wouldn't be done for a Detective Inspector to be caught over the limit'.

Roger sat down again. 'Yeah, I suppose so. I guess that invisible uniform of yours takes the shape of a strait jacket at times.'

'I suppose it does. It's a useful reminder of how one should behave.'

Roger gave a mock salute. 'Point taken.'

Both men smiled.

'Well, if we gotta go, we gotta go, but could I ask you one last favour? Could you give me a lift home? That's the one thing I really miss: my own set of wheels. I bloody hate public transport. It means mixing with the public, ugh.'

'OK, but let's be quick about it. I have a date with a spicy chicken, remember.'

Roger laughed. 'Lucky old bird.'

On leaving the pub, the fresh air had a strange effect on Snow. Although he had only drunk two pints of beer, the sharp cold mixing with the alcohol began to make him feel a little woozy. This surprised him but he was not too concerned. He felt pleasantly relaxed and less tense than usual and was happy to walk alongside Roger in quiet contentment while his companion chatted away.

As they approached the car, Snow's foot slipped on a patch of

frosted pavement and Roger grabbed his arm to steady him.

'Whoa, boy,' he cried. 'Are you all right?'

'Perfectly.'

'Fit to drive?'

'Indeed. I've only have a couple of pints.'

'On an empty stomach?'

'I'm fine.'

'Pleased to hear it.'

The two men resumed their walk to the car, Roger still holding Snow's arm.

Aware that he was not quite as clear-headed as he should be, Snow drove with extra care. Eventually, he pulled up outside the Chesil Bank flats, the illuminated windows of which spotted the blackness of the December night.

'I don't suppose I can tempt you in for a night cap, Inspector?' said Roger before giggling. 'But perhaps not. One more drink and you'd have to stay the night and that would never do, would it?'

Snow did not reply.

'Well, thanks for the lift, old boy. I'll see you and Mat on Saturday.' Roger leaned over and planted a kiss on Snow's cheek. Snow turned suddenly gazing at him, his face illuminated by the lights of the dashboard. With slow deliberation, he pulled Roger towards him.

When Snow got home later that night, there was an answer machine message from Matilda waiting for him. He sat in the unlighted sitting room and listened to it:

'Hello Paul. I'm sorry not to be able to talk to you in person. There is so much to say. I must apologise for being so distant, so distracted recently due to this Roger business. I have been very neglectful of you, I know. Been a bit of a bitch, if the truth were told. I'm so sorry. I hope you'll forgive me. Anyway, now he's moved out, I hope we can get things back as they were. You know… well I hope you know that I'm very fond of you. Please give me as ring as soon as you're able.'

Snow put his head in his hands and sighed heavily. What a particularly unpleasant can of worms he had just opened.

CHAPTER TWENTY FOUR

Lucy still needed alcohol to get her through the day and particularly the night. While, in one sense, she now felt, how could she phrase it, able to accept what she had done, she still was in pain and fearful. Very fearful. Especially of the nightmares, those dark dreams in which she re-enacted 'the terrible deed'. She would wake up trembling, her whole body moist with sweat. Then she would reach out for the vodka bottle.

It was late Saturday afternoon and, with the aid of alcohol, she had fallen asleep in front of the television only to be propelled into consciousness by the same horrific dream. Even awake, the dreadful squeals of the dying baby still rang in her ears.

'God,' she cried out. 'I thought you'd make this better. You were supposed to make this fucking better.'

She reached out for the vodka bottle and knocked it the floor, the contents gurgling out on to the carpet.

'No! No!' she screamed as she attempted to snatch up the bottle, but it was too late. It was empty. She moaned. How would she cope without the booze? The answer was simple: she wouldn't. She began to cry, her body heaving with sobs and she threw herself face down on the sofa, burrowing her face into a cushion while the television in the corner continued to burble.

Suddenly, a thought flashed into her mind. Her body froze, she stopped crying and gradually she pulled herself up into a sitting position. Her face was tense and determined. She had made a decision. With a dramatic gesture, she dragged her sleeve with some force across her damp face to sweep away the tears. With quick mechanical movements she went to the sideboard and checked her purse. It told her what she already knew. Well, that was not going to stop her.

The off licence was about three streets away, its brightly lit window shining like a garish beacon in the darkened street. There were several customers already in there perusing the shelves, probably, thought Lucy, getting ready to stock up for Christmas. She joined them, wandering around casually examining the stock. It was all an act of course for she had seen the display of spirits when she first entered; in particular the stack of vodka bottles near the door. Slowly, she gravitated to these and then picked one up and pretended to read the label. The assistant, a young girl about the same age as Lucy, took no notice of her. Then a burly fellow in a dark overcoat plonked three bottles of wine on the counter. 'I'll take these, love,' he announced in a gruff, friendly manner. The assistant smiled politely and turned all her attention to him. Lucy acted quickly. She slipped the vodka inside her coat and walked quickly to the door. Within seconds she was out on the street running and grinning. She kept up a steady pace until she was a few hundred yards from home.

'Clever girl,' she told herself as she caught her breath. It struck her that after the success of this little venture perhaps she would never have to pay for a bottle of booze again.

So pleased was she by the success of her escapade, that she failed to take much notice that her flat door was slightly ajar when she returned. She just assumed that, having left in such a determined hurry, she had forgotten to close it and lock it. 'That's what drink does to you, girl,' she grinned, moving into the warmth of the sitting room, holding up the vodka as though it was a trophy. It was then that she noticed the shadowy figure at the other side of the room.

She gave a gasp of surprise, nearly dropping the bottle.

'Hello, Lucy,' said the figure, moving forward into the light.

Initially Lucy was tense with fearful apprehension, but on hearing the voice and then seeing the face, she began to relax.

'Hello,' she said with a smile. 'What are you doing here?' But then as she spoke, the fear returned. It suddenly struck her that something wasn't right here. How had this person got into her flat and why were they waiting in the shadows for her return. This was creepy. No, it was beyond creepy. It was frightening. Something prompted her to repeat the question: 'What are you doing here?

This time there was no smile.

'I've come to give you something,' came the reply and the figure stepped forward, coming close to her. She only caught a brief flash of the knife before it entered her body and the final pain began.

In another part of the town, Paul Snow and Matilda Shawcross were seated around a tiny dining table in Roger's flat, while he carried out the final touches to the starter in the kitchen area only a few feet away. For different reasons Snow and Matilda felt awkward about this occasion. She was only there out of a sense of duty and to some extent guilt at the way she had treated her brother. Snow also felt guilt and was fiercely aware of the dark and crazy path he was now treading. He was here with his girlfriend, a woman of whom he was very fond, in the same flat as her brother, the man he had slept with only a few nights earlier. The scenario had all the ingredients of some bizarre Grand Guignol farce –

a farce which, he was only too aware, could turn into a tragedy at any minute. As an intelligent and sensitive man he loathed himself and was appalled that he had allowed himself to get into this position.

After receiving the answerphone message from Matilda, Snow had called her at work the next day and they had arranged to meet for a drink the following evening. Paul had intended to end the affair that night. He felt soiled and treacherous after the incident with Roger and he believed that the only decent thing was to separate from Matilda. It was folly to continue and so unfair on the girl. He had to admit now that he could not give her what she wanted and needed. His stirred up feelings for Roger had proved that once and for all. He had tried to live a lie and fallen at the first fence. But when they met Matilda was so loving and so happy to be back in his company that he could not face hurting her. Not just then. It would be too cruel – or that's what he tried to persuade himself. He knew he was being a coward yet again and only delaying the upheaval but he needed time.

'Simple but delicious, rather like me,' announced Roger, plonking two plates with a mixed salad starter down on the table in front of Paul and Matilda. They smiled at each other and then at Roger. God, thought Snow, this was like a bizarre Noel Cowerd comedy. And what made it worse was that Roger, oleaginous, smiling Roger, seemed to be enjoying it. My God, Paul thought, I could smash him in the face… or hug him to my breast and kiss him.

The salad stuck in Snow's throat.

'Well, that was quite pleasant, I suppose. But I hope that it was a one off. Roger needs to get on with his own life now and leave us in peace. What d'you think?'

Snow was driving Matilda home, hoping that she would not invite him in for bed and breakfast, when she made this observation.

'I agree,' he replied in the absence of anything else he could say.

'What Roger really needs is a boyfriend. Someone who can take him in hand while at the same time looking after him.'

Snow's hands tightened on the steering wheel but he said nothing.

'You OK?' she said.

'Tired. It's been a long hard week.'

'Not getting anywhere with these terrible murders?'

The mention of the murders reminded Snow of the other reason he felt stressed and mentally exhausted. For this uncomfortable evening where his personal life had turned into a nightmarish deceitful charade, the situation at work had slipped to the back of his mind. With Matilda's comment, it forced its way forward once more.

'I'm afraid there's been no progress at all.'

Matilda stroked his arm. 'Poor darling'.

Snow grimaced. That was the last thing he was. Duplicitous bastard queer would be nearer the mark.

Matilda had been very understanding when he dropped her off at home and he declined her invitation to come in for a coffee. He offered up the weak excuse of wanting to get a good night's sleep and she accepted it with grace.

On reaching home, Snow sat for some time in his sitting room in the dark feeling wretched. He had no idea what he was going to do about the Roger/Matilda situation. It seemed that whatever he did people were going to get hurt and he could find himself in the mire. He thought back over the evening. How Roger had seemed completely at ease, even amused by the situation. Quite clearly, the deceit was adding spice to his life. When Matilda had gone to the loo, he had leaned over and kissed Paul on the cheek and giggled and winked.

Like an arthritic old man, Snow dragged himself upstairs, undressed and got into bed. For the moment, sleep was the only answer to his problems. Sleep: the great escape.

Any plan to have a long lie in on the Sunday morning was scuppered by the harsh bellow of Snow's bedside telephone. It dragged him from deep slumber and continued its piercing wail as he rubbed the sleep from his eyes and pulled himself up into a sitting position. He gazed at the offending instrument. It certainly wasn't going to refrain from bleating until he answered it. The caller was obviously most insistent.

It was Bob Fellows.

His message short and sweet: straight to the point. 'There's been another murder. Looks like the same MO.'

Snow groaned. That was all he needed. Could things get any worse?

'Give me the address and I'll be there within the hour.'

Bob Fellows was having a quick cigarette outside the ancient block that housed the tiny flats where Lucy Anderson had lived when Snow arrived.

'Fill me in with the details before we go up,' he said rather more brusquely than he intended.

'Young girl, in her twenties, Lucy Anderson. Cut badly, in the same way as the others. It was the neighbour upstairs who found her. A Mrs Conroy, a widow. Claims to be sixty-five. And some, I'd say. She was taking her dog out for its early morning constitutional and she saw the girl's door open. She went inside and found her on the floor on the hearth rug.'

'What do we know of the girl?'

'Not much at the moment. She'd not been here long. Strange thing is, Mrs Conroy thought there was a baby. Said she's heard a baby crying but there's no sign of one. It was probably some loud pop music blaring out. You know what these old folk are like.'

'Anything else?'

'Not really had chance to look at her personal stuff yet for addresses, contacts etc. She'll have parents somewhere…'

Snow gave a heavy sigh and nodded towards the door. 'Let's go up.'

The tiny flat, stuffy and airless, seemed crowded with SOCOs. Snow had to squeeze past them to catch sight of the body. The girl was lying on her back, her knotted fists resting over her wounded midriff, which was caked in blood. Strangely, her face bore a serene expression, the lips almost curved into a smile and the glazed eyes gave no sense of panic or pain.

'McKinnon's been and gone. He was here in quicksticks. Caught him on the way home from a party.' Fellows murmured in Snow's ear. 'He said there appeared to be nothing new here. Just like the other ones, he said.'

The words seemed muffled and distant as though someone had placed cotton wool in Snow's ears. Suddenly his throat felt dry and his vision blurred. The girl's body began to shimmer before him. He had the strange sensation of being unable to move as though all his energy had been sucked out of him.

'You all right, sir?' Dull words in his ears. They echoed faintly as though someone had turned down the volume on his world. He moved his head slowly to face his sergeant whose features appeared to shift in and out of focus, his mouth opening and closing as muffled words escaped. Snow tried to speak, to articulate his thoughts, his great desire to leave this airless room, but the words wouldn't come. And then his legs began to buckle under him. They seemed to lose all rigidity and he found himself falling forward.

Suddenly, he felt a tight grip on his arm and his limp body being dragged towards the door. The curious faces of the other officers in the room peered at him as though seen through a misty distorting mirror. There was a dreamlike whirl of sensations and blurred images, his body jerking uncomfortably as he was propelled along. The next thing he knew, he was sitting on a wall outside, breathing in the cool morning air. Gradually, the world came back into focus.

'You OK, sir?' Bob Fellows peered at his boss with a concerned frown.

Snow found his voice again. 'What… what happened?'

'It looked like you had a bit of a funny turn. I thought you were about to faint. It was stuffy in there.'

It took Snow a while before he replied. 'Yes. Airless.' He shook his head in consternation. 'I don't understand…'

'I reckon a cup of tea and a bacon sandwich'll make you feel fine. I bet you've had no breakfast. That could explain a lot. You can't be looking at bloody corpses on an empty stomach. We can come back and have and look round later, when they've removed the body.'

Snow, his mind still in a mist and unsure of anything at the moment, nodded in agreement.

'Right, a cuppa and a sarnie it is. I know just the place.'

As Bob drove to the greasy spoon café for their tea and bacon sandwiches, Snow tried to work out what had happened to him in that room. As his thought processes gradually sharpened and returned to normal, the answer to the conundrum seemed clear and simple, staring him brutally in the face. Yes, the room was stuffy and crowded and yes he had not eaten breakfast but the main cause of his fainting fit was stress. Seeing the dead girl had

triggered something in his brain. The pressures in his life, held at bay by his normal stoical resolve, had broken through the barrier and swamped him. Here he was facing yet another murder victim and he had no idea how he was going to catch the perpetrator. He was lost, in a fog, all at sea, up the creek without a fucking paddle, without a clue. He was a useless copper! He could feel the hot breath of Clayborough breathing down his neck. And while this was going on, his personal life was spiralling out of control. He was involved, sexually, with his girlfriend's brother and even an idiot could tell him that whatever happened in this unholy triangle a great deal of shit would hit the fan at some point and there would be damage. And he would be to blame. Weak, stupid Snow. No wonder his brain had taken an avoidance procedure, prompting him to faint, a temporary but feeble escape route. With a tight grin, Snow resolved that this should not happen again.

After a mug of hot, dark brown tea and the very acceptable bacon sandwich, he felt much better physically. However, inevitably that dark shadow of concern lingered like an indelible stain.

'The colour's coming back to your cheeks, sir,' observed Bob cheerfully but without much conviction, still chewing on the remnants of his sandwich.

Snow smiled. "A cuppa and a sarnie' – your cure all remedy, eh?'

Bob nodded enthusiastically. 'That and a pint of bitter.'

Snow maintained the smile but added, 'I think we'd better get back to the murder scene. I'd like to have a look round.'

On their return to Lucy Anderson's flat, they discovered, to Snow's relief, that the SOCOs had gone, leaving a stoutly built constable on guard by the door. There was still the ghastly array of bloodstains on the sofa and the hearthrug where the girl's body had been and the smell of death lingered in the muggy air. Snow could not help but grimace as he gazed at the grisly sight.

'You OK, sir?'

'Yes. I'm fine. Let's have a look around, see if there is anything which might tell us something about Miss Lucy Anderson and her life, relationships etc. Some damned clue as to why anyone should want to kill the girl and why.' Snow was aware that his voice sounded strained and desperate but that was how he felt.

The two men moved around the tiny flat silently, opening drawers and cupboards, sifting through the wardrobe. Snow made a note of his surroundings, creating mental images for future reference. In one of the drawers in the kitchen cabinet, he found a photograph album. It was a pictorial history of the girl's life: baby shots of her in a pram and on the beach, pictures of her at school, at a party, with friends at a disco. But the last few pages were missing, torn out. It was as though Lucy Anderson was trying to deny her recent past. There was just one tiny loose photograph slipped into the plastic covering on the back cover. It was a blurred snap of a very young baby.

'Sir,' Bob's urgent voice broke into his thoughts. 'Look at this.'

Snow moved to the cramped bedroom where Bob was kneeling down, examining the contents of a large cardboard box. 'I found this stuffed right under the bed. It's full of baby clothes.'

Jigsaw pieces began slipping together in Snow's mind. 'You said the neighbour thought there was a baby?'

Andrews nodded.

'And I've just found a picture of a tot – less than six months old I should say.'

'But there's no sign of it now. Perhaps she had it adopted or maybe the father's got it. If it's hers.'

'We'd better circulate as recent a picture of her as we can get hold of to the press and make enquiries at the local hospitals. Someone should come forward to help…'

As he spoke the words, he knew the sentiment was fragile. Indeed someone should come forward – but often they didn't. People didn't want to get involved with the police. They didn't trust them like they did in the old days. It was easier to let sleeping dogs lie. Even the girl's parents may not want to identify themselves. The fact that she was living alone in a cheap flat could mean that there had been a rift in the family and her mum and dad had washed their hands of her. Snow knew for a fact that the notion of happy families in the modern world was a romantic concept.

'We'd also better see what the SOCOs found. There'll be her handbag and possibly other stuff. If there is a baby, I want to know what happened to it. And there is some urgency in the matter.'

When Snow arrived back at headquarters, he was feeling rough once more. His head pounded and his stomach churned. The greasy bacon sandwich sat uneasily in his gut. He gritted his teeth, desperate to ignore these feelings, but not quite succeeding. Bob Fellows was perceptive enough to note the change once more in Snow's disposition. 'You grab a coffee, sir, and sit down,' he said, 'while I get in touch with the chief SOCO and find out exactly what they dug up. Then we can have a powwow about our plan of action.'

Snow felt too weak to argue. 'Right you are,' he murmured, giving Fellows a gentle pat on the back.

Once in his office, he slumped in his chair and ran his hand over his forehead. It was damp with sweat. 'What the hell is happening to me?' He uttered the question out loud which prompted him to return in his mind to his own self-diagnosis. He saw himself rather like a balloon that had been filled full of air but maintaining a taut skin which was firm and resilient. This had allowed him to keep so many dark secrets to himself – strictly to himself - over the years. Not least were his sexual proclivities and his own desperate attempts to suppress and divert them. Now, through his own foolishness, he was in relationship hell. This, combined with the extra pressure caused by the total lack of progress in the current murder case, had caused the once firm skin of the balloon to rupture and the whole thing was deflating in an ugly fashion. He was deflating. It was as though his mind was telling his body that he had enough. It was not just a mental rebellion, but a physical one as well.

While this thought pierced his consciousness, there came a sharp rap at the door; but before he had a chance to respond, it opened and Chief Superintendent Clayborough entered. With one swift movement he shut the door.

'Sir,' said Snow, half-rising from his chair.

'For God's sake sit down man, you look awful.' The voice was harsh, unsympathetic. 'Are you sickening for something?'

'I'm just feeling a little off colour, sir.'

'Are you? Well, I heard about your little dramatic fainting fit this morning at the crime scene.'

'How…?'

'I have my spies. Very little happens around here that I don't know about.'

It'd be one of those bloody SOCOs no doubt, thought Snow. Telling tales to the headmaster in the hope of getting a gold star. Bastard.

'I just felt…'

'A little off colour. I know you said. Well you still look a bit off colour – or, if I may be frank, very much off colour.'

Snow pursed his lips. He knew what he wanted to say but he still had enough sense and reserve to hold back. He was sure there was more to come. He gazed at the stern features of the man before him. There was smouldering anger there. And Snow reckoned he was the target for it. It was unreasonable and unfair but that's what happens. You get upset and frustrated that things are not going your way so you kick the dog. It happens in all walks of life and the police force is no different. In this instance, he reckoned he was about to become the dog.

'In my opinion, Paul, you've not been functioning on all cylinders for some time. This is the fourth victim now and we're no bloody nearer nailing the bastard behind these murders. We're becoming a laughing stock. Incompetent plods. You've made no headway whatsoever.'

'You know yourself, sir, that random killings give you no real evidence to work on. Nothing to give us a lead. There is no real pattern – or no discernable pattern behind the crimes.'

'Discernible pattern!' Clayborough barked the phrase. 'It's your job to find one. Four people are dead already! How many corpses do you need to discern the fucking pattern?'

'You're not being fair, sir. We're doing our best.'

Clayborough pursed his lips and raised his brows in bitter disdain. He leaned forward over Snow's desk, thrusting his face forward. 'Then your best isn't good enough,' he said softly. 'While you are sitting at your desk, twiddling your thumbs, feeling a little off colour, our man will be out there carving up victim number five.'

Snow wanted to smash his fist into his superior officer's face and it took a great deal of self-control to prevent him from doing so. Snow knew Clayborough was being unfair and he knew that Clayborough was aware of it, too. He was taking out his anger and frustration over this case on a junior officer. As the man at the top, he couldn't appear to be the incompetent one. The one who was failing to catch the killer. A scapegoat had to be found – and Snow

now saw that he had been awarded this part. It was a role that was new to him and he was unsure how to act.

Snow opened his mouth to protest but before he had a chance to utter a word Clayborough dropped the bombshell. 'I'm taking you off the case.'

'What!' Snow's body stiffened with shock. It was as though he had been immersed in a bath of ice cold water.

'You've obviously got a health issue. You need some time off to recover. You are to take a month's leave to get yourself and your head together. We'll review the situation then.'

'You can't do this…' The words stumbled out as his mind tried to get to grips with what he was being told.

Clayborough gave a bitter smile. 'Oh, yes I can. I'll pass over the investigation to Crowther. He's a good man. He'll lead your team. I'll leave Fellows in place. He'll be able to bring Crowther up to speed.'

'This is so unfair.'

'In a situation like this fairness has no place. We have to catch a murderer. We have to protect the public. With four bleeding bodies at your feet, on your watch, you are in no position to talk about fairness. Do you think I'm going to sit up there in my office waiting to hear the news about the next victim and my officer in charge fainting on the crime scene? Go home, Paul. Rest and pull yourself together.'

With a swift movement he headed for the door where he turned back to face Snow. 'This isn't a suggestion, Inspector. It's an order.'

He slammed the door as he left.

Snow felt sick. His stomach retched and for a few moments his vision blurred. He felt unable to move from his chair so devastated was he by Clayborough's words – his instructions. While his private life was teetering on the edge of an abyss,

ready to plunge into disastrous freefall, he always had one rock in his life, one area where he felt secure and more than capable. Now that had been snatched from him. And snatched unfairly. Surely he had done all that was possible in this investigation to follow up what clues, what slender information, had been vouchsafed to him? No one could have done better. Could they? Well, obviously Clayborough thought otherwise. Of course, he realised that his dismissal had a political element to it. Even if the case had not been solved and brought to a successful conclusion, Clayborough would appear to be decisive and on the ball by replacing the incompetent officer in charge of the investigation with a new leader.

Snow sat slumped in his chair, staring into space, his mind virtually numb. He was tempted to head for the County and get drunk, but he knew this was a stupid idea and certainly would not, in the end, help matters. Getting pie-eyed was the last thing he needed to do.

Eventually he dragged himself to his feet. In a mechanical fashion, he snatched up a few personal possessions from his desk and then slipped on his overcoat and scarf. Just as he was about to leave the office two mental images flashed into his mind: they were fierce and invigorating. With a grim smile, he returned to his desk and dialled a number.

'Could I speak to Dr Mahendra Patel please? This is the police. Detective Inspector Snow.' He was told to hold on. It was quite some time before he heard the familiar voice. 'Paul, is that you? Long time no see.'

'Mahendra, I need your help.'

Five minutes later he exited the building in some haste hoping that the news of his enforced leave had not yet leaked out. He dreaded bumping into Bob Fellows. He had no idea what he would say to him. As it turned out, he managed his 'escape' (as he thought of it) without encountering anyone on his team.

He hoped to God that the little gleam of an idea would develop into a shaft of light. If only. However, little did he know as he drove out of the police station car park, that in another part of town things were about to get even worse.

CHAPTER TWENTY FIVE

It was the arrival of the post that morning that had started it all, that had pulled the bright and shiny rug from under Roger's feet. Having been in the little flat for only a few days and not knowing anyone in Huddersfield he wondered who on earth would write to him. He was not used to receiving post, apart from the odd advertising circular. Indeed this morning, apart from a couple of envelopes addressed to The Occupier, there was just the one letter which bore his name. It was a long thin envelope with a translucent window where the typed details could be read. At first, Roger was puzzled by it. Who would be writing to him in such an official way; unless of course it was something from the prison services? He thought he'd had done with all that. Why couldn't the bastards leave him alone?

However, the mystery was easily solved when he turned the envelope over and saw the firm's name printed on the back. Of course, it was about his interview. The one he'd had at haulage firm's offices just two days ago. This was quick. They had told him that they'd let him know within a week to ten days. He had thought the interview had gone well and he had conducted himself with the right mixture of confidence and deference. He'd left their offices convinced it was in the bag: the job was his.

Eagerly, he tore open the envelope with a smile and pulled out the sheet of paper with in. The message was brief and to the point; 'We regret to inform you that you have been unsuccessful...'

Roger felt as though he had been kicked in the stomach. He read the letter again: 'regret' 'unsuccessful'. There was no indication as to why – bloody why – he had been fucking 'unsuccessful'. No doubt it was because we don't want an ex-con soiling our smart office! We're an honest firm who only employ law abiding citizens – not gay old lags.

'Bastards!' he bellowed, and screwed up the letter as tightly as he could before hurling it into the far corner. 'Bastards!' he cried again, tiny tears of angry frustration starting to drip down his face.

He still needed to release more tension, so he snatched up his coffee mug and hurled it at the wall. It smashed, the coffee splashing everywhere, leaving the wall decorated with brown rivulets.

He retrieved the letter and un-crumpling it, laid it out on the table and re-read it once more, this time aloud. This was it then. He saw this rejection as merely the first of many. No one would employ him ever again. A man in his early thirties with no particular skills and with a prison record. He was on the scrap heap. Finished. Washed up. A bloody, fucking failure.

'We regret to inform you that you have been unsuccessful...' he roared at the top of his voice, before heading for the kitchen cupboard where he kept a bottle of gin. He banged it down on the table and stared at it for over a minute, feeling the hurt of the rejection burn into his soul.

At last he retrieved a glass from the work surface. 'Why not? he muttered. 'Why fucking not.' His voice was low now, but still filled with hardly restrained fury and hatred. He poured himself a large gin and downed it in two gulps. It burned the back of his throat and he coughed and gulped with the shock of it. When he recovered, he laughed. 'That was good. I reckon I'll have another.'

After pouring himself another drink, he slammed the bottle down again, this time on top of his letter of rejection.

In time the alcohol eased his mind, but played about with his thoughts. He was self-obsessed at the best of times and this, he was in no doubt, was not the best of times. He was alone, he mused. Alone, wretched and a pariah. He needed love and support. He needed someone to share his woes, ease his passage through this barren time. Someone to hold his hand and take him somewhere good. What was that old fashioned, biblical-type word? Ah, yes 'succour'. That's what he needed: succour. And he knew who he wanted, needed to provide it. His new best friend. His new lover. Dear old Paul. He would come to his rescue and provide that shoulder for him to cry on. And my god (another gulp of gin) did he need that shoulder now.

With this thought firmly in his mind, he made his way to the telephone and rang the police HQ in Huddersfield. On being connected, he asked to speak with Detective Inspector Paul Snow. This request prompted a series of questions which he found irritating: what was his name, what was the call in connection with etc, fucking etc. 'Look I just want to speak to Paul. It's a personal matter,' he growled into the mouth piece. There was a brief silence before he was informed that DI Snow was not available at present. 'Oh, go screw yourself,' he snapped before dashing the receiver down. No doubt his darling Paul was out there arresting some ne'er do well – just when he needed him the most.

He slumped down at the kitchen table once more and took another slug of gin. Things will have to be done, he thought, his brain completely succumbing to the effects of alcohol now. He needed Paul and that was the most important thing.

On leaving the police HQ car park, feeling like a naughty schoolboy who has been expelled, Paul began to head for the

Huddersfield Infirmary. The car park, as usual, was full, with some cars parked on grass verges and other places where vehicles should not be parked. 'The hospital is doing big business,' he observed sourly to himself as he parked in a disabled bay and placed the card reading 'POLICE' on his dashboard.

With some alacrity he entered the hospital and made his way past the cafeteria and down corridor three which had a temporary sign taped on the door announcing 'Dr M Patel's Surgery'. Halfway down there was a waiting bay where a small group of outpatients were gathered. They possessed glum and bored faces, staring gloomily into space. A young nurse approached Snow with a clipboard. 'Name?' she said. She was glum and bored also.

'I don't have an appointment,' said Snow quietly, holding up his ID card. 'Dr Patel is expecting me. I just need a few words with him on an urgent matter.'

'Well, he's seeing a patient at the moment. You'll have to wait. He should be free in about five minutes.'

Snow joined the tableau of waiting patients, naturally adopting their dispirited demeanour, staring blindly into space. In less than five minutes a large middle aged lady with flushed features wobbled out of Dr Patel's consulting room clutching a sheaf of papers.

'You can go in now,' said the nurse, tapping Snow on the shoulder.

Dr Mahendra Patel was a tall, very good looking Asian with extraordinary brown eyes that radiated intelligence and perception. He grinned broadly as Snow entered and rose from his desk throwing his arm out in greeting.

'My dear Paul, this is such an unexpected pleasure. We have not seen each other in many a long day.'

Snow nodded, shaking Patel's hand. The two men had met during one of Snow's investigations and had become friendly on

a casual basis. Snow had even attended Patel's wedding two years earlier but since then they had seen little of each other.

'I gather this is not a social call and you do not want your bowels examining,' Patel said mischievously.

'I need some information, I'm afraid and I reckon you are my easiest channel for obtaining it.'

'I see. Well, I'll do what I can, but it will have to be quick, I have several patients waiting outside all wanting to know how their bum is doing.' He chuckled.

'I know this not your department but I need to know something about a girl who I believe gave birth in this hospital probably within the last year.'

Patel chuckled again. 'You are right, it is not my department. Babies are not my area of expertise, but I reckon I know people who could help. Tell me more.'

'There isn't more to tell. The girl's name is Lucy Anderson, a single mother. The child was white, possibly a little girl.'

Patel lifted the phone. 'I'll get on to the midwifery department. They should be able to help.'

'Good man.'

Snow waited patiently as Patel spoke to his colleague on the phone and then waited again while records were checked. Some five minutes later Patel replaced the receiver and handed Snow a sheet from his notepad.

'That's all the details I could glean, old chap. A girl, Lucy Anderson, aged nineteen, gave birth four months ago. As you say, a single mum. No record of parents. Probably deceased. No record of the father of the child either. Sadly that is not uncommon these days. She gave birth to a baby girl, born prematurely. About two months early. Religion: Roman Catholic. Address given was given as Ramsden Buildings. Any use?'

'Could be. It certainly clears one matter up. Thanks for your help. I'll let you get back to your patients.'

Dr Patel stretched out his hand for another friendly shake. 'It was good to see you again – however briefly.'

'Ships that pass in the night, eh. I hope you and Surinder are well and happy.'

Dr Patel beamed. 'We are. You must come round for a meal sometime.'

'That would be good.'

'Indeed, next time you give me a ring, make sure it's for some social occasion, eh?'

Snow made his way back to the car, his mind moving various pieces of information around in his mind, searching for anything that glimmered with a promise. Now it was time for him to go home and have that drink.

When he arrived home he saw that there was a familiar vehicle parked outside his house. As he pulled into his drive, the occupant of the car got out. He was carrying a manila file.

'Hello, sir,' said Bob Fellows with less than his usual ease.

'Bob, what brings you here?'

The sergeant looked embarrassed and shifted awkwardly from one foot to the other. 'I'm sorry about what's happened, sir. It's bloody ridiculous... No one could have done any better, got any further with the case than you... And then they go and give it to that idiot Crowther, I mean...'

Snow thought Bob's indignation was touching but also rather comic.

Snow smiled. 'Come inside and have a drink.'

As Snow poured a glass of lager for his sergeant, Fellows slapped the file down on the kitchen table. 'I've spent the last hour photocopying various documents and photographs relating to the case. They're all in here. I reckon just because you are officially off the investigation it doesn't mean that you have to give it up, does it?'

'Exactly my thinking,' said Snow, with a sly smile. He opened the folder and sifted through the material. 'That's very good, Bob. Very thoughtful. Thank you. This stuff will be useful to me'.

'I'll keep you informed about how things are going… off the record like.'

Snow nodded. 'Of course. That will be appreciated. Actually, I've made a little headway myself.'

'Already?'

Snow's smile broadened. 'Already. I've visited the hospital and I can confirm that Lucy had a four month old child – a little girl.'

'What about the father?'

'No record of him. He'd obviously done a bunk before the birth.'

'So where is the baby now?'

'That is a good question. Perhaps Inspector Crowther will come up with the answer.'

Fellows rolled his eyes in response to this observation. 'And bacon sandwiches might fly,' he grunted before taking a long swig of his lager.

'The baby angle is interesting but it does not really give us an insight into the motives for the other murders.'

'That's our bloody holy grail isn't it?'

'Absolutely. That link still eludes us.'

Bob drained his glass and touched the manila file. 'Well, I hope this stuff helps. It's often the case that if you go over things, you spot something you missed the first time around.'

He drained his glass, patted Snow gently on the shoulder and headed for the door. 'I'll get out of your hair. Don't worry, sir. I'm sure we can sort this out between us.' His features shifted briefly into a tight grin.

Snow felt immensely touched by this demonstration of kindness and loyalty. It had surprised him and the fact that it had increased his sense of humility.

'Much appreciated, Bob,' he said, hoping that his tone and steady gaze added greater eloquence to his feelings than the simple expression.

After his sergeant had gone, Snow sank down onto a kitchen chair. His legs seemed to crumple under him. Suddenly he felt very tired. A wave of exhaustion engulfed him. It had been a hell of a day but he had, until now, apart from his fainting fit, managed to keep the stress of it at bay. Until now. Left alone in his own silent kitchen, his reserve crumbled. He actually felt like crying, but his eyes remained dry. He sat like a melting statue for some fifteen minutes, his mind awhirl with thoughts and flashing images of moments he had lived through the last few days. It was like a grotesque and distorted newsreel. Eventually, with a snarl he banished them, clearing his brain and, standing up, he made a determined effort to shake off the malaise.

Self-pity, capitulation to despair and maudlin thoughts were not going to help him dig himself out of the hole he was in. Constructive thought was his only life-line. A fragile one, he admitted, but that was all he had. His eyes caught sight of the whisky bottle on the work surface. It shimmered before him in temptation. It was a temptation he knew he had to reject. Instead he lifted the electric kettle and replenished it from the tap, the noise of the water drumming inside filling the room. Just as it was coming to the boil, the doorbell rang.

Snow grimaced. A line from Dorothy Parker came to his mind and he found himself murmuring it as he made his way to the front door: 'What fresh hell is this?'

On opening the door, he found a hunched distressed figure standing there. It was Matilda. She had been crying. Snow adjusted

this observation. She was crying. He eyes were red, her mascara had run and she was shaking with emotion.

On seeing Snow, she stiffened, her body grew more erect and her features toughened. With great speed her arm arced forward and she smacked him hard across the cheek.

'You bastard,' she cried. 'You fucking bastard.'

CHAPTER TWENTY SIX

A few hours earlier that day, Matilda had driven away from school with a splitting headache. She was tired and ready for a hot bath and a gin and tonic. The Christmas term was always the most draining one of the school year. Not only were there the carol concerts to organise, the Christmas parties and the nativity play to set in motion and oversee, but there was the increasing skittishness of the kids as the festive season took hold. This year, of course, the pressure had been added to by the re-emergence of Roger in her life and the rippled effects this had upon the comparatively calm waters of her life. And then there was Paul. She was perplexed as to where this relationship was going to go. Especially now after their mini-rift. She was very fond of him, maybe even a little bit in love with him, but she was unsure of his feelings for her. Even in his passionate moments, there was always something reserved about his behaviour as though he was afraid to reveal the true Paul Snow completely. It was a puzzle and she did not yet know how to solve it. Of course, her coolness towards him when she was first dealing with Roger had not helped. She hoped things would not only get back on an even keel but indeed progress over the Christmas period.

Their first Christmas together.

The traffic was particularly bad this evening. The slow stop/

start progress in the December early evening darkness, penetrated all the while with startling bright headlights of oncoming vehicles, increased the ferocity of her headache. She was in a really bad way when she at last pulled into the drive of her house. It was only when she had switched off the engine that she noticed that there were lights on in the hall and sitting room. Her immediate thought was burglars, but then it was bit early in the day for nocturnal thievery and then she reasoned, with a sinking feeling, it was more likely to be Roger. Unfortunately, he still had a key.

Remembering this, she groaned. That's all she needed - burglars would be the better option. With some trepidation, she entered her own house. She had thought that the apprehension she felt rising within her was a thing of the past after Roger had moved out. More fool her, she thought grimly.

She discovered him sprawled on the sofa, fast asleep, a glass held limply in his hand. It appeared to contain gin. It wasn't water, Matilda was sure of that. She dumped her coat and bag down on a chair and went through to the kitchen. It was clear to her that when sleeping beauty woke up he would need a strong dose of black coffee.

As she waited for the kettle to boil, she considered the various possibilities that had brought her brother back to her house, somewhat worse for wear with drink. Something must have happened to 'upset' him. It usually didn't take much. His horse had come last, a potential boyfriend had turned him down … or… Of course. It was the job, wasn't it? she reasoned. His first interview and his first rejection and so boo hoo let me get drunk and cry on my sister's shoulder. She was fairly certain that was the scenario.

She stirred the coffee slowly, mesmerised by the little coin of creamy foam spinning on the black surface. Tired as she was, she certainly was not in the mood to be Roger's Florence Nightingale,

offering him sympathy and ministering to his ego. She returned to the sitting room, extracted the glass from her brother's limp grasp and placed the mug on the coffee table before shaking his shoulders with some force.

'Come on, wake up, Roger. Get some coffee down you.'

After another shake, his eyes fluttered erratically and then slowly opened wide. It took him a few seconds to establish where he was and, perhaps, Matilda thought wryly, who he was. With a groan, he pulled himself up into a sitting position.

'Coffee.' She pointed to the mug on the table, the creamy coin having disappeared.

'Thanks,' he croaked and raising the mug to his lips took a long gulp.

'Ouch,' he cried. 'That's bloody hot.'

She ignored him and sat down. 'What are you doing here?' Her voice was hard and angry. She wanted him to be in no doubt that she was very pissed off to come home and find him in her house, soused on the sofa.

'I need to talk to you.'

'What's wrong with the telephone?'

He shook his head wearily. 'This is too important… too sensitive for the telephone.'

'Sensitive…?' She didn't like the sound of that.

'I'm in a mess.'

You have been for years, she thought, but kept it to herself. 'I gather you didn't get the job.'

For a moment Roger look confused and then his eyes brightened as comprehension returned. 'The job. Yeah. I mean no, I didn't get it. They turned me down. Ex con cannot be trusted.'

'They didn't say that.'

'They didn't have to.'

'Well, you knew it wasn't going to be simple. Jobs are not that easy to come by these days even...'

'Even for those without a prison record, eh?' There was real anger in his voice now and his hand shook so much the coffee sloshed over the rim of the mug.

Matilda decided not to retract the thought. 'Yes, even for those without a prison record. You have got to face facts.'

To her surprise, he began giggling, giggling in an unstable way. 'I reckon it's you, sis, who's going to have trouble facing facts.'

What the hell did he mean now? She raised her brows in silent query.

'I may be fucked up but it's not all hunky dory in your garden either.'

'What are you getting at?'

'Lover boy. Little Pauley.'

'Paul, what about him?'

'Indeed, sister of mine, good question: what about him?'

'For God's sake drink your coffee, sober up and get out of here.'

'You've got to know. For both our sakes, you've got to know.'

'Know what?' Matilda felt decidedly uneasy now and something told her things were suddenly going to get very unpleasant.

'Your boyfriend. Paul. He's like me.'

'What do you mean...?' the sentence faltered on her lips, for she felt she knew the answer to the question.

'He's a pansy. A queer.'

Matilda gave a laugh. It was false and melodramatic.

'I am afraid it's true.'

'You're talking nonsense.'

Roger shook his head. 'Do you think I would make this up just to hurt you? I'm not that big a bastard. It's the truth. Paul and I are of the same breed, I assure you. I should know: we've slept together.'

As the sense of these words stabbed at her brain, Matilda gagged and her stomach convulsed. She thought she was going to be sick or faint. Her whole body seemed as though it didn't belong to her any more. Her distress came from the full acceptance of Roger's claim. She believed him. Why would he lie? Why would he lie about this? It explained so many things.

She began to cry. Silently and without any dramatic motion, the tears poured down her face. Roger rushed forward and knelt by her chair. 'I am so sorry. I know it's horrible but it is best you know. I think he has feelings for me and I have for him.'

'I don't want to know! I don't want to know!' she snarled, her body beginning to heave with emotion. 'Get out. Get out and never come back! Do you hear me? Never. Never. Never!' The voice rose to an hysterical pitch now which unnerved Roger. He pulled back from her, rising to his feet.

'We never meant to hurt you...'

Matilda gripped the arms of her chair, her nails digging into the fabric. 'I'm sure you didn't. I'm sure you didn't give me a second thought. Either of you.' She paused, the fury dissipating for a moment, replaced by a brief sob. 'It is true,' she said at length, 'isn't it? This isn't one of your fantasies. A cruel lie?'

Roger shook his head. He suddenly felt very sober and wretched. 'I wouldn't... My God, I wouldn't. If it's any consolation, I did the chasing but...'

'What a fool I've been. How stupid...'

'No, no. Paul never meant to deceive you.'

Matilda gave a bitter chuckle. 'You're going to tell me that he was deceiving himself. Burying his true nature.'

Roger gave a shrug of the shoulder. 'Trying to at least.'

'Go now.'

'And never darken your doorstep again,' he said in a failed

attempt to be flippant.

'Yes. I meant what I said. But do me one last favour.'

'Of course. If I can.'

'Leave Paul alone tonight. Don't go running to him. I need to see him. There are… there are questions I need to ask. From tomorrow he's yours, but… leave him alone tonight.' Tears began to roll again.

Roger nodded. 'Very well. If I could use your phone to call for a taxi…'

Matilda nodded.

'I'll get them to pick me up at the end of the street. I'll be out of your way in a trice.'

Within five minutes he was gone and Matilda was alone. She hadn't moved from her chair as though paralysed by the shocking truths that had just been revealed to her. Had it really all been a sham? Had Paul just used her to create a fiction, representing a heterosexual face to the world to cover up the truth? It seemed so cruel. *He* seemed so cruel. And strange. They had been close, intimate and loving towards each other. But then, she considered, not quite as close, intimate and loving as she would have liked. Examining their relationship under the brutal magnifying glass provided by Roger, she could see the weaknesses, the cracks, the fallacies. The more she reviewed the affair, she saw with fresh eyes how she had romanticised their friendship, pushed it along, Paul following uneasily in her wake. She saw it all now. The horrid truth. Of course, it was partly her fault but in truth Paul was the real demon. He had known it wasn't right. He had known that it was a pretence. Even if it was self-delusional, he had placed his own considerations first. He hadn't given a thought for her feelings at all.

He was a bastard. With this one idea burning fiercely in her mind, Matilda rose from her chair and with great deliberation moved out into the hall, retrieved her coat and bag and left the house.

Paul was a bastard and she intended to tell him so.

The taxi dropped Roger off at his flat. When the driver had first asked him where he wanted to go, he had been tempted to ask to be dropped somewhere in town. He would seek out a bar and continue drinking but he realised that was a pointless activity. He had drunk enough today. He felt strangely sober now and he wanted to remain that way. What he had done to his sister had been hurtful and he knew she would not forgive him, but it had cleared the decks and, he hoped to God, that it had provided a chink of an opportunity for him to be happy. Maybe with Paul's help and love, he could survive, make something of himself again. He knew he would have to do a lot of persuading and cajoling, but he was good at that.

Once indoors he slumped down on the sofa with nothing stronger than a cup of tea. He switched on the television and stared at it, mesmerised by the shifting patterns on the screen but he wasn't watching it. His tired mind roamed over the events of the day and wondered what he would say to Paul the next time he saw him.

CHAPTER TWENTY SEVEN

Snow took a short step backwards with the force of the slap. His face stung and his eyes watered, but he did not mind. He guessed immediately why she had done that. Her face revealed it all. She knew. She knew all about him. Roger had told her. It was all there to be gleaned from her tear-washed angry visage. He accepted that he was fully deserving of her fury and, indeed, very much more. Having delivered the blow, Matilda seemed on the verge of turning on her heel and leaving. Snow reached out and grabbed her arm.

'No,' he cried. 'Don't go. Don't go like this. We need to talk.'

'There is nothing to say.'

'I think there is. Please.' He let go of her arm and placed his hand on her shoulder. 'Please. I beg you. Please.'

Some moments later, they were in the sitting room. Matilda had refused to take off her coat or sit down. She stood close to the door, her emotions now calmly held in check.

Snow stood awkwardly by the fire place. 'I am sorry…' he said lamely.

'What for? Deceiving me. Pretending that you felt something for me when it was all a lie, a bloody pretence. A cover for you. For your real passions. Old Chinese proverb: man with girlfriend is not queer.'

'It wasn't like that.'

'Wasn't it? Well, then, perhaps you'll tell me what it was like.'

'I didn't mean to hurt you or deceive you. I thought it was different with you. The only person I was deceiving was myself.'

'You are a homosexual.'

Snow cringed at the word. It was horrid and clinical. But he could not deny it.

'Yes,' he said reluctantly. 'I suppose that is my label. I have tried to subvert my sexuality for years. I certainly would not have got where I am in the police force if it were known I was… I was that way. It's not been easy. I didn't ask to be like this. There's no choice in the matter, you know. For the most part I have been celibate. I had been for some time when I met you. I suppressed my emotions and got on with my life. The police work was my life. Then, suddenly, there was you. You were so warm, kind… I liked you a lot and when you seemed to like me … well, I wondered. Maybe...'

'Maybe,' she repeated the word, but she turned it into a sneer.

'Maybe it could work. I wanted some companionship in my life.'

'You were lonely and couldn't risk kissing a man. Is that it?'

Snow shook his head. 'I cared for you. I still do.'

'But not in that way, eh? Not in the way it matters to a woman. Your stomach must have been churning when you made love to me.'

'No, no. You've got it all wrong.'

She gave a bitter derisive laugh. '*I've* got it all wrong? That's bloody rich. Where on earth did you see our relationship going, eh?'

'To be honest, I tried not to think that far ahead.'

'No. You were too wrapped up in protecting yourself – maintaining the charade.'

'Oh, Matilda, I never saw it as a charade.' He slumped down in a chair and dropped his head into his hands. He had run out of words.

Gazing at him, Matilda felt a pang of sympathy. 'I suppose I've had a lucky escape. Well, we've both had a lucky escape.' Her tone was kinder now, more reflective.

He looked up at her. There were tears in his eyes. 'Please believe me, I never meant to hurt you.'

She didn't reply, but her eyes told him that, despite her anger, she accepted what he said.

'What are you going to do about Roger?' she asked.

He shook his head. 'Nothing. That was an aberration. A weakness. It was a physical thing – lust if you like. But it can go nowhere and I don't want it to.'

'A physical thing! Can you hear yourself? My God, Paul, you've made an almighty mess of things.'

'I guess so. All I can do is say sorry and hope you can forgive me.'

'I'm too angry at the moment to contemplate forgiveness. You knew right from the start that you were experimenting and using me as a guinea pig. It's a bloody big ask to forgive you for that. You are a sensitive, intelligent human being and fully aware what you were doing. It was selfish and cruel. You never really considered my emotions at all.'

Snow hadn't seen things in this way, but expressed harshly by Matilda, he knew that she was right. Her condemnation of him and his motives were valid and justified. He shook his head in self-disgust.

'I'm going now Paul. Please do not try to contact me. I never want to see you again. Is that clear?'

He opened his mouth to protest but he realised immediately

that it was pointless. Matilda was right. There would be no point in prolonging matters. He nodded his head. 'Yes. Yes, it's very clear.'

Without another word, she swept from the room and a few seconds later he heard the front door slam. The sound echoed around the silent house. A wave of sadness swamped him. He was aware that in his own way he had cared for Matilda. More than he had previously realised. She had become part of his life and had brought some warmth and humanity into his rather barren existence. And now she had gone. And it was all his fault. His stupid fault.

Gradually, he was being isolated. His girlfriend had gone and his job was slipping away from him. God knows what Roger would do when he rejected his advances. His anger and petulance might easily prompt him to broadcast to the world that his sister's boyfriend was a closet queer. Snow knew that such an exposure would complete his ruination. He would be finished on the force and he would be finished in the town. Quite simply he would be finished. The slamming of that door was symbolic: it was like a door closing on his past life, sealing it off forever.

CHAPTER TWENTY EIGHT

It was about three o'clock in the morning when Snow gave up all hope of getting any sleep that night. His mind was a viper's nest of thoughts. They wriggled and thrashed around in his brain until his temples throbbed and his head ached. Bright, garish images paraded in quick succession before his inner eye: Matilda's tear-stained face, the twisted corpse of Lucy Anderson lying amid a scattering of baby clothes, Roger's beguiling lips, twisting mechanically into an infuriating rictus grin. And Chief Superintendent Adam Clayborough, striding from his office and slamming the door with such ferocity that the walls crumbled away leaving a barren rock strewn landscape. With a groan, he switched his bedside light on and surrendered. It was no sleep for him that night – and the way he felt, never again.

With the slow movements of a geriatric, he donned his dressing gown and padded downstairs to the kitchen. He made himself a cup of strong black coffee and slumped down at the table. After a while the fierce hot brew revived him somewhat. The file Bob Fellows had brought him was still lying there untouched and unread. Idly, he flipped back the cover. Why not? He thought. Why not give it a perusal? For God's sake I've nothing better to do and it might take my mind off the demons in my head. This thought encouraged him. He was, he knew, never happier, never more relaxed, never more himself than when he was involved in police work. It was unsentimental, analytical, involving objective thought and action. He was able to lock away all personal concerns while wearing his Detective Inspector's hat. God knows how long he would be able to do that – so let's get on with it. He took a large gulp of the scalding coffee and focused his eyes on the material in the file.

Most of the forms and reports were very familiar to him - indeed, he had penned a number himself – but it was good to reacquaint himself with all the material, allowing him to gain a detailed overview of the murders. He was able to connect the pattern in his mind, although he still could not observe a connecting link between all four incidents. Then he came to the last murder, the young girl Lucy Anderson. Briefly he had a flashback to his fainting episode in her flat that morning and his mouth ran dry at the recollection, but with a determined effort he squeezed it from his thoughts. He told himself that it was of no consequence now and that he must concentrate on the job in hand. It was when he began reading the list of contents in the girl's handbag that he began to grow excited. One item stood out from the rest. One item that seemed to solve his dilemma. One item that may well provide him with that much searched for connection. One item that may well indicate the identity of the murderer. It certainly showed him that he needed to speak to someone urgently.

When daylight first squeezed its way into the December sky, it revealed that it had snowed in the night and left a slushy white covering over the land. Errant flakes still spattered against the window pane and Snow could hear car engines out in the street revving hard in the slippery white stuff. He suddenly realised that he was hungry – he'd not eaten for nearly twenty four hours –

so he made himself some breakfast: a couple of boiled eggs and toast. Then slowly he carried out his morning ablutions. He knew that he could not set off too early for his destination. He didn't want to drag the man from his bed. Once he was dressed, he made himself another cup of coffee and listened to the news on the radio. It was after noon when he set off.

It had started snowing again with some force and the traffic was sluggish. He tried to be patient and careful, despite his eagerness to reach his destination as soon as possible. Once again he ran his theory through his mind trying to fit his suppositions in with the known facts and educated guesses to see if it really created a credible scenario. It had seemed so clever and clear the night before, but now in the grim, bleary light of day he was not so sure. What the hell, he had to try it out. There was nothing to lose, was there? He had taken risks in the past which had proved successful.

His desire to drive faster was quelled by the sight of a shunting accident. Three cars had slithered into each other on the icy slush. Their owners, snow bedecked silhouettes, were standing by their damaged vehicles exchanging details. Snow resigned himself to being the safe tortoise this morning, rather than the careless hare.

Eventually, he reached his destination just after nine o'clock. St Joseph's church looked very festive with its white winter dusting and the coloured lights of a Christmas tree illuminating the gloom of the porch. On leaving his car, Snow observed a figure, starkly black against the bleached out background, bending low with a large shovel clearing the path. He grew erect at Snow's approach. It was the church warden, Brian Stead.

'Come to give me a hand have you? I've got a spare shovel.'

'Another time perhaps,' said Snow pleasantly.

'Might not be needed at another time. No time like the present.'

The gruff, humourless tone clearly indicated to Snow that Stead was not indulging in light banter. He really was serious about recruiting the policeman's services to help clear the path.

'I need to speak with Father Vincent rather urgently.' He made a move to pass the church warden and head for the church door.

'You won't find him in there,' grunted Stead.

'Where is he?'

'He'll be at the vicarage. Like as not in his tool shed at the bottom of the garden. He's there most afternoons pottering about. God's work comes later.'

'Where…?'

'Back of the church, beyond the gravestones. You'll see the path, unless it's snowed up. Vicarage is through the gate there. You can't miss it. You being a detective like.' He smiled mischievously.

Snow nodded his thanks and moved on. He made his way as directed and indeed the path was snowed up. It had drifted up against the church wall and the wet soggy slush came over his shoes as he walked. He passed through the gate down the virgin snow of the path leading to the door of the vicarage. He rang the doorbell but there was no reply and so reluctantly he made his way around the back of the property where he espied a substantial garden shed, the light from its illuminated window spilling a golden rectangle onto the smooth white bedecked lawn.

He trudged through the snow and knocked hard on the wooden door. Moments later it was yanked wide by the occupant. Father Vincent peered at the dark figure on the threshold. 'Why, it's you, Inspector,' he said at length. 'Come in. Come in. What on earth brings you here on such an inhospitable wintry day?' He took Snow's arm and led him to a chair close to where there was an electric fire with two orange bars humming with heat.

The room contained a work bench and a set of woodworking

tools fixed neatly to the wall. There was what appeared to be a table leg clamped in the vice on the edge of the bench and an abandoned chisel lying nearby. 'I'm just making some minor adjustments to one of the chairs in the vestry. It's rather old and wobbly,' the priest explained.

Snow nodded.

'Now, I was just about to have a cup of tea and from the greyness of your complexion, I reckon you could do with one also.' He pointed to a small table with tea making equipment at the far side of the bench. 'All mod cons here, y'know.'

Snow really didn't want to get involved in the rigmarole of a tea ceremony but he knew that it would be easier to go along with it. 'A little milk, no sugar,' he said politely.

Father Vincent poured some water into a large, old fashioned electric kettle. He then plugged it in and organised two mugs with tea bags. While the kettle began its boiling process he turned to Snow with a gentle smile. 'There, we'll soon have a brew. I'm down here most weekday afternoons, doing a little work on the bench or just reading – the newspaper or a light novel. It's a kind of haven. There's nothing in here connected with my calling. No church related stuff. That's all in the vicarage. I believe in trying to stand back from religion for a while. It helps one gain a perspective on the world and, in a way, helps me do my job all the better. I think sometimes people forget that priests are human beings with personal interests and concerns of their own.' He ran his hand down the chair leg and then extracted it from the vice. 'A little woodwork is very therapeutic. It allows me to escape into my own little world for a while. Do you have a hobby or a pastime, Inspector, something that helps you shrug off some of the worries and responsibilities of police work?'

'Not really,' admitted Snow.

‘That’s a shame. The stress of the job can eat away at you.’

‘You feel like that sometimes, do you?’

Father Vincent paused to pour the hot water into the mugs. ‘Sometimes,’ he said softly. He finished making the tea and without another word handed Snow his mug.

He sat down opposite the policeman with a sigh. ‘So, as I was saying: what brings you here, Inspector?’

‘You,’ said Snow simply.

‘Me. I don’t understand.’

‘I’m not sure I do either, but I thought you’d be able to help me.’

‘If I can, but I doubt it. I am assuming you are referring to the unfortunate deaths of Sammy Tindall and Frank Sullivan. Well, I’ve told you all I know.’

‘I am not convinced that you have.’

‘Oh. Do explain.’

‘Let me present you with an overall picture.’

The priest gave a gentle sardonic smile and nodded his head. ‘By all means.’

‘In the last six weeks there have been four murders in this area. We are convinced that all the crimes were committed by the same person. The modus operandi was identical in each case and forensics informs us that the weapon was the same: a large serrated knife – maybe a kitchen knife. Now, two of the victims were regular parishioners of yours: Tindall and Sullivan.’

‘That is more or less correct, although I would perhaps quibble at the description ‘regular’. They certainly visited the church on occasion but I would hardly call them regular.’

‘O.K. But you took for confession from both of them.’

‘They came to see me, yes. I told you all that.’

‘And you assured me that nothing they said would aid me in my investigation.’

'Yes.'

'Now I come to the other two murders. First there was Simon Barraclough. A fellow who had no religious convictions whatsoever.'

'I know nothing about him.'

'Well, we'll put him to one side for a moment and turn to the most recent victim: Lucy Anderson. I have reason to believe that she visited your church also, probably for a confession.'

Father Vincent took a sip of tea before responding. 'Really. What leads you to this conclusion?'

Snow leaned forward in his chair and pulled a sheet of paper from his pocket. It was the picture of Christ taken from Frank Sullivan's locker. He held it up in front of the priest. 'A copy of this was found crumpled up very tightly in the handbag of Lucy Anderson. She didn't come by it by accident. She either took it from the church or more likely she was given it. Lucy was an unmarried mother, another sinner in the eyes of the church, in your eyes...'

Father Vincent held up his hand to protest but Snow carried on. 'Now Lucy's child appears to be missing. A little girl. We do not know what has happened to it but it is not beyond the realms of possibility that a lone, depressed mother with a demanding infant on her hands may do something very drastic – may in fact have done something very drastic.'

The priest's eyes widened in shock. 'Good gracious, what on earth are you saying?'

'I think you can guess. And, in fact I believe that you know. I believe that this young girl came to you because she was desperate and despairing. She came to confess her sins. What had she done with her baby? Where is it?'

'I don't know. Really, I have no idea.'

'Why not?' Snow's voice was raised now and tinged with genuine anger. 'She came to you for confession, didn't she? So what did she do with the baby?'

Father Vincent stared at Snow for some moments, his mouth moving slightly as though he was about to speak but was unsure which words to use. Eventually he replied in a hesitant hoarse whisper. 'I can't tell you.'

'Why not?'

There was a long silent pause before the priest replied. 'Because I didn't ask her.'

Snow slumped back in his chair with a frustrated sigh. Nevertheless now he knew he was getting somewhere. His hunch was working out.

'What *did* she tell you?'

'You know I cannot...'

'For Christ's sake...'

'Yes, for Christ's sake.'

Snow rippled with anger and stabbed a finger in the priest's direction. 'Don't give me that. It's not Christ and your so-called vows to him that are you are protecting. It is yourself'.

'What on earth do you mean by that? I think you are making statements here that could get you into trouble.'

'Don't you threaten me, Reverend Father. You see, I know what you've done.'

Father Vincent rose quietly from his chair, placing his mug of tea on the workbench. 'I think that you had better go now.'

Snow shook his head. 'I don't intend to go until I've managed to secure a confession from you. You know all about confessions don't you?'

'Why, you're mad!'

'Mad, no. I've been a little slow I grant you, but with a little hard thinking and the extra piece of evidence provided by that picture found in the girl's handbag, I reckon I've now got a clear idea of what has been going on.'

Strangely, the priest smiled. 'And what has actually been going on?'

'Murder. Murders perpetrated by you.' For a brief moment the image of the street lamp outside his office came to his mind. The garish artificial light snuffing out, easing the night back into its natural state, just as the murderer had done. Just as Father Vincent had done: reducing the harshness of the world by eliminating it. Disposing of sinners and moral bankrupts, cleansing society. What had been a vague notion, a hunch, now, as he was talking, was becoming crystal clear to Snow.

'Inspector, I really don't know what has led you to this crazy idea but I am afraid you are terribly wrong. I am a priest. A man of God. It is my calling to save souls and not take lives.'

'An ideal mask for a murderer. I remember something you said to me when we first met: 'If I could, I would wipe all the pain and sin from the world.' I believe that is what you set out to do. In your own rather twisted way. Even Brian Stead, your church warden, observed that you struggled at times to have sympathy with the people who came to you for confession.'

'That is only human.'

'Possibly. But what you did next is not. I think that the terrible outpourings that you have to endure in the confession box turned your mind. Why should these creatures be excused punishment? Isn't that what you thought? They had committed the most horrendous sins and for a few Hail Marys they were free of guilt and punishment. Take Sammy Tindall, for example. He beat his wife. He was a brute and a drunkard. Surely he didn't deserve to live. You were in no doubt that despite his bleatings for forgiveness you knew that he'd be back seeking it again.'

The priest nodded. 'Certainly. Once a man has raised his hand to a woman, he cannot stop.'

'So you stopped him. In your eyes he did not deserve to have a life and so you ended it.'

Father Vincent shook his head. 'This is fantasy.'

Snow continued. 'Then there was Frank Sullivan. His crime was greater. He was a paedophile of the worse kind. He had sex with his own daughter. No doubt he sobbed and cringed in that confessional box while you offered him succour, while your own stomach was turning over as he relayed the foul details of his transgressions. The man was vermin, wasn't he? He needed to be trodden under foot. Or stabbed in the stomach until dead. When Lucy came with her tale of woe, you realised you had found yet another victim: an unmarried mother who had done something terrible to her baby. What had she done? Left it on a doorstep somewhere or worse still, done away with it? It's too late shaking your head now. You will have to tell. You will have to tell all in a court of law. Three sinners came to you and you took it into your head to be their executioner. To rid the world of this sinful scum.'

Father Vincent clasped his hands together and smiled indulgently. 'I am afraid you are living in cloud cuckoo land, Inspector,' he said softly, without a hint of emotion. 'All you have told me is nonsense and more importantly totally lacking evidence. And one other thing. What about the Barraclough fellow? He was not a parishioner of mine. I never met him. He has never been near my church.'

It was Snow's turn to smile now. 'Indeed. That was your really clever move. To kill someone with whom you had no connection. A stranger to you. But he was a well-known sinner, generally recognised as a piece of shit on the heel of society. Well deserving of your knife. In killing him, you threw away any suspicion of a link between the victims and your church - and you. It bought you a little more time. You knew that eventually the police would catch on to the pattern you were creating but you confused matters significantly by killing Barraclough. However, I am sure if we get the forensic boys into the vicarage they'd find enough stuff in there to ensure you'd spend the rest of your life inside. Where is the knife, the murder weapon? Is it in the kitchen drawer? Or maybe you keep it in here.'

'Quite the little Sherlock Holmes, aren't you?' There was no smile on the priest's face now. 'I have to congratulate you. You seemed to have worked it out very well. All on your own, eh? No police back up, I see.'

'That can easily be arranged. To be honest, I wasn't quite sure I was on the right track until I came in here this morning.'

'And then it all became clear to you, eh? Very well, I won't deny it. Not to you anyway. Obviously, I have not been clever enough. I have to congratulate you, but it won't do you any good, you know. The theory works but you have no proof. Nevertheless, well done. I was driven to it, you know. I have always been susceptible to callings – that's why I entered the church – but religion is feeble when it comes to cleansing society, improving the morality of the people. What I saw as a benevolence, a way of easing a sinner's pain, in practice was merely a licence for them to go out and do it all again. There would always be a cop out provided by the priest – the priest who could not tell anyone about the darkness and malevolence that poured from their lips. No one gave me an absolution. I had to live with those grim recitals, buggery, violence, murder, theft, abuse. Those tales can corrupt, taint a soul in time. In God's house, I had to endure tales from the pit.'

'So you thought you would take the law into your own hands. Be your own cleansing agent.'

'Those people did not deserve to live. I chose them carefully. They had offended Our Lord – in fact anyone's sense of decency. The idea of my blood rites came to me when I was attacked myself by some young ruffian on my way home from visiting a sick parishioner. Attacked, beaten and had my wallet stolen. And then that very night, less than an hour after the brat had assaulted me, he was run down by a speeding car. That was justice, wasn't it? God's work. If God could sanction such an outcome, it was a sign for me. A sign allowing me to blot out the vile individuals who have inflicted pain and misery on others. They all deserved to die.'

'You could be right but it is not given to you to be their judge and executioner.'

'If I did not do it, who would?'

'Isn't it God who decides such things?'

'Maybe he has. As one of God's anointed, perhaps he has given me the power and authority to carry out his work. A disciple of His justice.'

'You don't really believe that.'

'Perhaps I don't. But I shall carry on with my work.'

'It ends here.'

Father Vincent laughed out loud. 'You mean that you're going to read me my rights - 'anything you say may be used in evidence etc etc'? Don't be so foolish. I am afraid you're not going to arrest me. Look, it has been somewhat cathartic for me to admit what I have been doing and why. Strangely, it has been my kind of confessional. Yes, I admit I murdered those four people. I did it because they had offended humanity, let alone God, by their actions. They had soiled their own lives as well as their victims. Why on earth should they go on breathing the same air as decent

honest folk? They shouldn't – but they would have done if it hadn't been for me. For years I have sat cooped up in the confessional box listening to the crude and pathetic outpourings of these creatures, from the grubby and petty to the grotesquely immoral. It damages one's soul and mind after a time. It is like holding a microscope up to nature and what you observe is disheartening and disgusting. I know I can only make a small difference – but it is a difference.'

The words were expressed calmly, rationally and there was no note of madness in the expression or in the priest's features, but it was in the objective manner in which he delivered his little sermon that Snow caught the sense of the man's insanity.

'But now you know... I am afraid...' The priest's features darkened and his stance stiffened.

Sensing danger, Snow rose from his chair. As he did so the priest moved with remarkable swiftness and released the chair leg from the vice on the workbench. Before the detective knew what was happening, Father Vincent brought the chair leg down on his head in a rain of blows. Snow raised his arms to protect himself but it was too late. The weapon cracked hard against his skull several times. He fell backwards, his head seeming to explode with bright coloured lights. A further blow brought darkness and with a groan he slumped to the floor unconscious.

CHAPTER TWENTY NINE

Father Vincent was aware that he had to act swiftly and move the body before Snow regained consciousness. He didn't want to kill him here, not on his own territory. That would be both extremely dangerous and foolish. He knew exactly where the deed was to be done. He had already sussed out several locations ideal for dumping a body, although he had not contemplated that it would be a policeman. This killing was not one of his blood rites, but a necessity to allow him more time to carry on with his calling. With great precision he set about preparing his victim for the move. Using gaffer tape, he sealed up Snow's mouth and then bound both his hands and feet tightly with thin rope. To complete the job, he slipped a small potato sack over the policeman's head.

The priest paused a moment to catch his breath and admire his handiwork. He knew that he had been extremely fortunate that the Inspector had called on him alone to voice his suspicions. Had he turned up with his sergeant and other police in tow, the game would have been well and truly up. God had been good to him. However, he was fully aware that he was not out of danger yet. He had to get the body to its final resting place without being seen. Kneeling down, he felt inside Snow's overcoat and after a brief search found what he was looking for: his car keys. The priest assumed that Snow had left his car in the parking area just outside the church gates. He would have to go to the vehicle and drive it around to the rear of the vicarage in order to stow the body in the boot without being seen. That would mean leaving the unconscious Snow alone for about five minutes. It was a risk, but surely a minor one. The fellow was trussed up like a Christmas turkey, the apt analogy bringing a brief smile to the priest's face. If he regained consciousness, he couldn't make a sound or move.

There was no time to consider the matter further. He had to act quickly. Slipping on his overcoat and hat, he locked the door and trudged through the slush down the garden path, around the vicarage towards the front of the church. It was still snowing and feathery flakes settled on his coat and hat as he walked. He recognised Snow's car parked near a street light and swiftly made his way towards it. What he did not notice was the figure of Brian Stead standing in the porch. He was positioned well back in the shadows, but the glow of his cigarette was discernible in the gloom had Father Vincent glanced that way. Stead often stood there for his regular 'fag break' but he was meticulous in catching the ash in the palm of his hand and slipping the final tab end into his overall pocket to dispose of later.

Father Vincent's rather furtive gait intrigued Stead somewhat and he took a step forward in order to obtain a better view of the priest through the fine net curtain of snow. He even raised an eyebrow of surprise when he saw him unlock the policeman's car and get inside. Soon the lights of the vehicle sprang into life and the engine revved up. In a stately fashion, the car slid away into the snowy gloom. That was strange, thought Stead. Very strange, in fact. However, he gave a gentle shrug and puffed on his cigarette and blew the smoke into the shadows. It was nothing to do with him. He knew his place and knew what was best for him. It was the Yorkshire man's mantra: see all, hear all and say nowt. He had survived this long in life by being vigilant while keeping his mouth shut. Silence cannot hurt you. Whatever Father Vincent was doing with the copper's car was none of his business, he mused as he doused the cigarette and slipped it into his overall pocket. 'In fact,' he murmured to himself, 'I didn't see it. I saw nothing.' And with a tight, satisfied grin, he made his way back into the church.

On returning to the workshop, Father Vincent Andrews was delighted to discover that Snow was still unconscious and his body was exactly as he had left it. This made it all the easier for the priest to transfer him to the boot of the car. Hauling the inert policeman over his shoulder, he made his way down the little path which led him to the narrow lane behind the workshop where he had parked the car. Unceremoniously, he dumped Snow's body into the boot and slammed the lid shut. He stood for a while, catching his breath while the snow still swirled around him like the tiny flakes in a glass globe.

It was nearly over.

It was early evening as Father Vincent neared Beaumont Park, the Victorian recreation gardens on the north side of the town. The roads were quiet, most motorists having headed home early in order to avoid getting stuck in the snow. The priest drove slowly with care. It would be disastrous if he got stuck in the snow. As he approached the park on the quiet suburban street which ran parallel to it, the car began to slide and the steering grew resistant to command.

'Come on,' snapped the priest leaning over the wheel, urging the car to take a straight route as the engine groaned in protest. The front end slithered to the left in response and then the whole vehicle glided across the road bumping into the curb, close to a parked van mummified in snow. Father Vincent uttered an oath and wrenched the wheel savagely, while revving the engine. With an angry whine, the car shuddered for a moment before pulling away from the pavement and then slowly and jerkily returning to right side of the road.

Father Vincent realised that his forehead was doused in sweat and his heart was beating a tattoo inside his chest. It was as though the weather – nature – was attempting to stop him carrying out his plans. Was this a sign from God? Surely not. It was just the bloody weather. Bad luck – that's all.

Slowly, as if in slow motion, the car edged its way towards the T-junction by the park gates. Gently he manoeuvred the car towards the side of the road, just beyond the gates, and parked it. He sat back for a moment and sighed while waiting for his heartbeat to return to normal. He switched off the lights and sat in the darkness for five minutes, watching the falling snow bloom everything in sight with a soft, white-edged brilliance.

Eventually, he got out and checking that he was indeed a lone figure in this arctic landscape, he retrieved Snow's body from the boot. As he hoisted him over his shoulder, the priest was aware of faint stirrings of consciousness evident in his burden.

As swiftly as he could, he carried the body though the park gates and turning left headed towards a seat shelter where he dumped the policeman down on the wooden bench. He arranged him into a sitting position before pulling the sack away. Snow's head lolled gently and his eyes flickered as though he was gradually taking the slow pathway to wakefulness.

Father Vincent smiled. Indeed, he did want his victim to be fully awake for the final act in the drama. Picking a handful of snow up, he rubbed it into the policeman's face. His features twitched, the eyes widened and slowly began to focus. The priest repeated the procedure. This time Snow began to cough and splutter behind his gaffer tape gag.

'Welcome back to the land of the living. Temporarily anyway.'

Snow tried to say something but his words were muffled by the tape, emerging as groggy inarticulate grunts.

'Don't bother trying to talk – trying to talk your way out of your fate. I believe you are a good man really, but you are also an obstacle. You have got in my way and in order for me to continue in my work you have to be… eliminated. It's a pity, but there it is.'

He moved away from Snow and reaching into the lower folds of his overcoat he retrieved the long, serrated kitchen knife from the inner pocket there.

On seeing the knife, Snow began to wriggle wildly but his desperate actions were in vain. His bonds were too restrictive and within seconds, Father Vincent had plunged the knife deep into his stomach and with great forced dragged it upwards, ripping the flesh and severing various internal organs. He then withdrew the knife and plunged it in again.

Snow's body shuddered for a while as though caught in a ferocious fit while his legs flexed outwards, twitching violently. Then suddenly all movement stopped.

The eyes closed for the last time.

Father Vincent dipped the blood-stained knife in the snow and wiped it on Snow's jacket.

'Sweet dreams… may flights of angels sing thee to thy rest,' he said softly, kindly with a gentle smile.

Then, with a sigh of relief, Father Vincent made his way to the park gates and the long trudge home in the snow.

He entered the darkened house and shivered, kicking the damp snow from his shoes. Damn, he thought. He had forgotten to put the central heating on timer. Now it would be an hour before the property was reasonably warm. He grimaced and slammed the door shut. Oh, well, such is life, he mused as he clicked the kitchen switch, filling the room with harsh fluorescent light. After seeing to the central heating boiler, and plugging in the kettle, he went to the sink and extracted the polythene bag from his overcoat pocket. From this he unsheathed the long knife. Despite the fact that he'd wiped it earlier, the blade still retained traces of blood. He dropped it into the sink and turned on the tap. The water gushed over the knife, the blood reluctantly diluting and then spiralling away. He watched fascinated as the red turned to pink and then slid from view down the plughole crater.

Well, he supposed, the evening had been successful – after a fashion. He wasn't happy that he'd had to deviate from his plan and kill for no other reason than to protect himself. He knew that this had been essential, but it was essentially the waste of a body. However, the killing did provide him with the opportunity to resume his planned course, his blood rites, and take many more unworthy lives.

He dried the knife on a tea towel and returned it to the kitchen drawer where it belonged. Everything in its place; a place for everything. Sloughing off his wet coat and draping it over a dining chair, he made a cup of tea and, grabbing a couple of digestive biscuits, he wandered into the sitting room. After turning on the television, he slumped in a chair. He took a slurp of tea and sighed. He hoped there was something relaxing and entertaining on television he could watch. He'd had rather a tiring evening.

Why not explore another of David's recent thriller titles, *The Scarlet Coven.*

New York 1936. Leading New York detective Simon Finch has received an unexpected inheritance and left the force to pursue his dream of becoming a writer.

But a true detective is never far from finding trouble...or trouble finding him...

A stranger approaches Finch in the Algonquin Hotel, asking him to help find his sister who has disappeared. When he later

visits the man's hotel room he discovers that he has been murdered - stabbed with a dagger decorated with strange markings. As Finch investigates further he discovers recently acquitted crime boss Fats Molloy is mixed up with the man's murder and the missing sister.

The trail leads him to an occult bookshop ...has the missing woman been kidnapped by a group of Satanists, The Scarlet Coven?

Joining forces with a black private eye, Patrick Murphy, who is also investigating the cult, they endure a series of wild adventures and close calls with demonic forces as they seek the truth about the mysterious leader of the Coven...and the nefarious plans for death and mayhem...

David Stuart Davies is an author, playwright and editor. His fiction includes six novels featuring his wartime detective Johnny Hawke, Victorian puzzle solver artist Luther Darke, and seven Sherlock Holmes novels, the latest being Sherlock Holmes and the Ripper Legacy (2016). His non-fiction work includes Starring Sherlock Holmes, detailing the film career of the Baker Street sleuth. David is regarded as an authority on Sherlock Holmes and is the author of two Holmes plays, Sherlock Holmes: The Last Act and Sherlock Holmes: The Death and Life, which are available on audio CD. He has written the Afterwords for all the Collector's Library Holmes volumes, as well as those for many of their other titles. David has also penned three dark, gritty crime novels set in Yorkshire in the 1980s: Brothers in Blood, Innocent Blood and Blood Rites. He is a committee member of the Crime Writers Association and edits their monthly publication Red Herrings. His collection of ghost and horror stories appeared in 2015, championed by Mark Gatiss who said they were 'pleasingly nasty'. David is General Editor of Wordsworth's Mystery & Supernatural series and a past Fellow of the Royal Literary Fund. He has appeared at many literary festivals and the Edinburgh Fringe performing his one-man presentation The Game's Afoot: an evening with Sherlock Holmes & Arthur Conan Doyle. He was recently made a member of The Detection Club.